SPIRIT SEEKER

The Kassandra Leyden Adventures

"the unknown won't leave her alone!"

JEFF YOUNG

eBooks

Pennsville, NJ

PUBLISHED BY
eSpec Books LLC
Danielle McPhail, Publisher
PO Box 242,
Pennsville, New Jersey 08070
www.especbooks.com

ISBN: 978-1-942990-69-7
ISBN (ebook): 978-1-942990-17-8

Interior Design: Danielle McPhail
Sidhe na Daire Multimedia
www.sidhenadaire.com

Cover Design: Mike McPhail, McP Digital Graphics

Art Credits - www.Shutterstock.com
Steampunk Girl © Irina Braga
Creepy graveyard with old tombstones © Unholy Vault Designs
Ouija Oracle © Katja Gerasimova

CONTENTS

In the reign of Edward, the third of his name,

the great plague known thereafter as

The Death, came over the land.

His most glorious majesty took up his people

and peoples of other lands and crosst the sea to

the New World, there to found New Britain.

DEFENDER OF THE DEPARTED

WHEN THE LEG KICKED, KASSANDRA JUMPED. HER MENTOR, LEHVOI, caught her eye, tipping his head in question. She pushed the probe linked to the static jar down harder and this time both of the frog's extremities floundered. However, Kassandra wasn't looking at the interior of the dissected creature any longer but at its dark eyes. She blinked. That wasn't possible, because the frog was lying on its back. She felt something at the corner of her mouth as if she'd run her tongue over her lips. Snatching off her gloves, she put her fingertips to her mouth and felt a spark leap up to meet them.

The eyes of the frog that were now staring at her were from an immaterial specter of the animal. The experience was like looking at an optical illusion. From one direction, there was a splayed corpse and from another the beady stare. Then she caught the shining reflection of her fingertip. A glistening coat of quicksilver lay over the pads of her fingers from where she'd touched her lips. The distorted image of her wide-eyed visage stared back at her. In the reflection, something moved behind her.

Dropping her hand, she turned in time to catch a glimpse of a figure in a dark cloak walking around her chair. When the other passed in front of the glass doors of the liquor cabinet, Kassandra observed that it cast no reflection. How many apparitions was she seeing? The human figure came to stop, standing over the frog. The long slender fingers of one hand came to rest on the amphibian's head. Something about them captured her attention a fleeting moment. Before she could tell what, the apparition's other hand reached out to her. Kassandra could feel the grip that settled on her forearm and she drew in her breath to scream. Just as suddenly as the vision occurred, she became aware that she was still seated in the leather armchair in the study of the folly on her father's estate. Lehvoi stood over her, his hand gently rocking the chair as he stared into her eyes.

"Are you all right, my dear?" he asked concern roughening his voice.

Before she answered, Kassandra brought her hand up before her face and stared at her fingertips. The mirrored illusion was gone.

Unknowingly mirroring the spirit, Lehvoi reached out, stopping himself just before he caught Kassandra's hand. She did her best to stifle a smile. While he was a brilliant mentor, Lehvoi was a bit of a germaphobe.

"It was ectoplasm. I know you've never seen it before. I..." he stopped and looked down at the floor, gathering his thoughts. Hooking a foot through the legs of a nearby stool, Lehvoi pulled it over and then sat down on it in front of her. He ran a hand through his unruly mop of brown hair as if gathering up his thoughts with his fingers. "I hoped that you might one day demonstrate the abilities that your mother had. Now, I need you to understand, Kassandra Leyden, that no matter what happens, what you have is a gift—a marvelous gift. You have an ability to see things that others will never experience."

A bell rang and they both turned to see Wexfield, her father's manservant standing in the doorway. Lehvoi swiftly came to his feet. Wexfield proffered her mentor a small silver tray bearing a white card. Kassandra immediately caught the change in Lehvoi's expression when he glanced at the card. He turned back to her and sighed. "I am so very sorry, Kassandra. I must take care of this. There is someone who has come a long way to see me. This will only take a moment and then we can continue our conversation. Please wait and I shall be right back."

When Lehvoi left with Wexfield, all Kassandra could see of the waiting visitor was the back of his tweed jacket. Their shadows passed by the windows of the top floor of the folly and came to stop on the balcony. She realized where the men were standing was exactly the same direction that the apparition of the frog and the stranger in the cloak had faced in her vision. Only then did she realize what she'd seen on the hands that caressed the frog. Adorning one long, slender finger of the left hand had been a familiar ring, a moebius twist of gold—her mother Anastasia's ring.

Unsettled, Kassandra pushed herself out of the chair and made her way over to the window. The angle of the outdoor shutters made it difficult for her to see the men on the balcony. She resisted the urge to pull the heavy velvet curtain away from the corner and peer out around the mount of the shutter, afraid that the movement would attract their attention. Instead she crept forward and turned her head, brushing aside her red ringlets she laid her ear against the cool glass. As she began to make out voices, she noticed how badly the hand steadying her against the glass shook.

She'd never known her mother's whole story—and father was certainly not going to tell her. He did his best to wipe those memories away with an omnipresent glass of whisky. All Kassandra knew was that when she was quite young Mother had gone away. She vaguely remembered Father telling her over and over that her mother would be back soon and better than ever. Anastasia had returned, but there was a marked difference. She went out at all hours and strange people came to speak to her in whispered conferences. It was as if her adventurous father had traded places with her now-mysterious mother. Anastasia no longer followed Casimir Leyden's lead. In fact, the two were often at odds, the least things sparking prolonged arguments. Five years ago Kassandra's mother had stormed out and never returned. Father refused to speak her name again and began drinking with a vengeance. If Kassandra had seen her mother's shade, then the worst was true. Somehow, perhaps deep inside, she had always known. When she glanced at her hand on the window, it no longer trembled. Closing her eyes, she leaned harder against the glass, striving to hear.

"What you're asking for is unreasonable." That was Lehvoi; she could pick out his nasal voice easily and imagined his ever-present, lace-edged handkerchief dabbing at his forehead. "I do understand the nature of the issue. You have good reason to be concerned about the safety of his Majesty and the possibility of any attempts on his person during the Royal Progress. But..."

"The Southrons are restless now. Mexateca are staging revolts in the south. The withdrawal of our adjutants and militias and the abandonment of our old plantations has given them notions. The days of indentured servitude has left them many memories and most of what they remember makes them less than pleasant."

The stranger had a deep voice that carried despite the clandestine nature of their meeting. Perhaps they felt safe here on the third floor of the folly tower at the edge of the woods on her father's estate.

"I understand and I, for one, am deeply concerned about His Majesty's safety. The Directorate has been most generous to me and I appreciate the support that I have received. But, I cannot rush things. I am fully aware that you want to interrogate the three Southron spies that were recently captured. If only you hadn't let that magistrate become so damnably inflamed with righteous furor that he ordered their immediate execution, we might be having a very different conversation right now."

"Can you do it?" What the other voiced wasn't truly a question, rather a gruff challenge.

"Don't be a fool, if you believed for one second that I couldn't wrest the information from those poor, dead bastards, you certainly wouldn't be annoying me now. It will take—" Lehvoi hesitated. "It will take time. I mean how cooperative would you be if you'd recently been strung up in the courtyard and left for the birds to pick at? I have to convince them that I'm an impartial voice, that I had nothing to do with their suffering before they trust me."

"There is no time. We need to know now."

"Oh, why on Earth am I explaining it to you? Suffice it to say that you will have your results. I can secure what I need tonight from Potter's Field and then I will begin my work. I will, perhaps, in consideration of what I'd mentioned, have to become more creative, Minister."

"Get me what I want. I don't care how. Just do it, Lehvoi, or you might be hanging from a tree soon yourself."

Kassandra's head came away from the window with a jerk. Lehvoi had to be talking to a Minister from the Directorate of Security for New Britain. And, by their conversation, he was interrogating the dead; there was no other way for her to interpret what she'd heard. The conversation she'd just eavesdropped upon could very easily get her arrested, interrogated, disappeared, or worse. Scrambling back, she fell, her legs briefly tangled in her crinoline, her knees tenting up her blue dress. She swallowed hard, gasping for her next breath. Then she realized that she could no longer hear the men talking.

Grasping the end table near her, she pulled herself up to her feet. There was no way she could face Lehvoi now. She was certain her guilt would be obvious no matter how disingenuous she might try to be. Kassandra's eyes roved about frantically until they came to rest on the nearby fainting couch. Of course, someone who had just undergone the experience that she had might be overwhelmed. Some rebellious part of her couldn't believe that she was going to feign an attack of the vapors, but her common sense swiftly overruled the dissent. She curled up on the couch hugging a pillow to her.

As she lay there, eyes closed, her mind raced in all directions. She'd had her suspicions about her mother's abilities. There was a certain direction in Lehvoi's tutelage that tended toward the realms of the inexplicable. Was he grooming her to be her mother's successor? Had Lehvoi taken advantage of her natural curiosity? After all, she'd mounted quite an offensive against her father's indecision to have him taken on as a tutor—with, of course, the understanding that Wexfield would be an appropriate chaperone. Never mind that Wexfield, after a short period of time had removed himself, once he was more assured of Lehvoi's intentions, to wander about the folly during the hours of her instruction, occasionally dusting, straightening, and smoking her father's cigars, filched from his humidor.

Kassandra's thoughts were interrupted by Lehvoi's returning footsteps. She lay there, doing her best to breathe evenly and fought the desire to bite her lip. There was a rustle of cloth. She expected that he was crossing his arms.

"I should have known. Such an experience was surely too much for you to take in all at once. Perhaps it is best I let you sleep it off," Lehvoi sighed.

She heard him moving away and then the soft closure of the chamber's door. She started counting to herself, half-heartedly wondering what would be a safe amount of time. At around two thousand, Kassandra heard the hinges of the door protest. She cracked an eyelid only to find Wexfield bending over the remains of the earlier experiment. He held the limp body of the frog by one of its hyper-extended legs as far as possible away from himself and marched to the nearest dustbin. The pungent scent of camphor once again reasserted itself in the room. Holding as still as possible, she listened to him cleaning up the study's large mahogany desk. He cursed briefly and she wondered if he'd gotten a shock from the probe she'd used on the frog's cadaver. That should teach him to fool about with the static jar. Wexfield stopped puttering about. When she heard the doors of the study click closed Kassandra gave herself another five-hundred count just to be sure.

With her eyes closed, she felt herself sliding away from reality. Once again the frog sat before her staring at her with its dead eyes. It felt as if she were falling forward into those dark pits. When her gaze tipped downward she wasn't standing on polished floorboards, but rather dead, sodden leaves. A large white door loomed over her. Her outstretched hand came to rest against the cool marble surface of a mausoleum. The graveyard, how had she come to the graveyard? A splashing sound caught her attention and when she looked past the side of the building she spied something writhing among the reeds. Long, scaled whips thrashed in the swamp. Was there a nest of snakes there?

At the sound of a huffing exhalation behind her, Kassandra turned and then fell backward against the mausoleum as the latest, inexplicable manifestation loomed over her. Tubes sprung from the sides of its head and steam rolled out from the cylinders at the bottom of the mask. The monstrosity cocked its head to one side as it stared down at her. She could see her open mouth reflected in the smoked glass mask it wore. Kassandra felt the heat of the steam on her face, but oddly there was no moisture to it. Disoriented, she took a step back only to find herself lying down instead of standing up. When she sat up from the fainting couch late-day sunbeams slanted through the windows of the folly to rest on her.

Tonight Lehvoi would be going into the graveyard after the remains of Southron spies. She cast a glance in the direction of the dustbin. Maybe like the frog, Lehvoi would need to be with the body to contact the departed spirit. But Potter's Field wasn't laid out in orderly plots like the cemetery with its stately mausoleums. It was a patchwork of mass graves and half-rotten wooden crosses where the criminal and the unclaimed found their final resting places.

Leaning against the curled back of the fainting couch Kassandra stared off into the direction of the graveyard until she caught a glimpse of a figure down below walking in that very direction. Surely Lehvoi was gone by now... The figure halted its progress only once to turn toward the tower folly, the dark hood obscured the face but the figure was familiar. Kassandra gasped as the phantom turned on its heel and plunged among the live oaks to disappear from sight, its black cloak billowing behind it. *Mother...* Kassandra pushed to her feet and raced toward the door. It had to be Anastasia once again and if she was going to follow Lehvoi, Kassandra would follow her mother.

After convincing Wexfield she wasn't feeling up to dinner and asking him to make her apologies to her father, she retired to her room. Or rather she went within, drew the door shut, and immediately began to prepare. Kassandra dove into her gigantic wardrobe, pushing her way through the masses of dresses feeling about in the depths. Upon securing a handle, she pulled her large steamer trunk out into the light. At the bottom she found her father's old aviator jacket. She wasn't sure when she'd stolen it from his closet, but she kept it close, because it reminded her so strongly of him before he changed. The stained leather would camouflage her well in the darkness. Further exploration brought forth a skirt of similar hue that she exchanged for the blue satin dress she currently wore. She found a pair of woolen tights and drew them on hoping that they might keep her warm in the early spring air. There was only one more thing to secure before sneaking out.

For once, Kassandra was glad that only her father and Wexfield lived in the giant manse. She worked her way from shadow to shadow as silently as she could manage. At the entrance to the main hall, she stopped and briefly looked over her shoulder, convinced that Wexfield would make an un-welcome entrance. Breathing a sigh of relief when there was no sign of the butler, she slid along the wall until she came to the door of the trophy room. The stuffed heads from her father's hunting expeditions lined the circular room as she ghosted across the floor intent on the long, thin box sitting on the mantelpiece. Flipping open the lid, she reached inside for a muslin-wrapped bundle containing her father's dueling pistols. Glancing to either side, she slid it into the front of her flight jacket, cautiously closing the lid on the box. In moments she was out of the room, then racing down the hall and opening a side window, she slipped out into the night.

Under the low-hanging branches of the live oaks, Kassandra stopped to take stock of the moment. She reached into her jacket and pulled out the bundle and unwrapped the pistols. Taking a moment to fill the striker pans and load powder, wadding, and a bullet into each, Kassandra once again gave thanks to her eccentric Uncle Aleks who let her do such unbecoming things as firing guns. Also wrapped in the muslin at the bottom was another prize: her father's hunting knife in its leather sheath. This she tucked into the band of her skirt and then pulled down the edge of the jacket. The pistols went back into the front of her jacket and she pulled the leather togs closed. She then stooped to gather up a handful of dirt, rubbing it over her face and her father's jacket before brushing aside a beard of Spanish moss. Kassandra stepped past the live oak and into the wooded plot.

Once she'd passed through the edges of her father's property, she found herself on one of the long levees. Her home, Amphyra, sat on the delta of the largest river in all of New Britain. The city fought a constant, slow-motion war against the encroaching river with a series of earthen dikes and locks on the canals. Just as the sun fell low on the horizon, she found her way to the low districts of the city. Kassandra hoped the limited light would aid her disguise as she hurried along. She desperately wanted to avoid pulling the dueling pistols on any of the rough-looking men and boys that slowly walked past her, their heads invariably slumped downward, feet shuffling them along.

When she looked down from the top of a small rise, the roadway ahead wound through an alley of leaning old houses. Its terminus was lost in a mass of rolling ground fog that rose from the perpetual damp of the graveyard. Two things were immediately obvious: the light bobbing about in the distance among the mausoleums, and the figure in black standing beneath the iron gate of the cemetery. Kassandra took a deep breath; after so long, she wasn't about to keep her mother waiting. She stepped forward, staying in the shadows as much as possible, the chill mist condensing on her cheeks and dewing her eyelashes.

A long time ago, she'd come here to picnic at the family mausoleum. Most of the cemetery sat on a small hillock with the ever-present swamp bordering the southern edge. Near the back was the long, flat area of Potter's Field where the criminal, poor, and unidentified were laid to rest without the care and ceremony of those whose mausoleum's kept them safe from the ground-water's swell. The figure in black had turned from the main gate and instead hurried south along the stone wall that bordered the plot. Kassandra followed the apparition hoping it was leading her to another entrance and that Lehvoi was suitably involved in his pursuits that he would not note her arrival.

After a brief run to the shadows cast by the wall, Kassandra made her way along, clinging to its side. The wall ran south, down away from the upraised land of the middle of the cemetery. Turning a corner, she felt her feet give way and tumbled down a small embankment to end up in the reeds, the water lapping about her knees. She pulled herself through the muck and back onto the shoreline. Her skirts a sopping mess, Kassandra waited breathlessly, listening to the sounds of the night, praying that Lehvoi had not heard her. After a few moments, her panic subsided and she considered the wreckage of her dress. Well there was nothing for it she decided, pulling her father's knife and hacking away half of the sodden material and the underskirt. The end result coming to just above her knees was a quite a bit less than decent and by no means fashionable, but now she could once again walk and run if need be. She poured the water out of her shoes and wrung what she could from her stockings before proceeding onward.

A quick check proved that the pistols were mercifully still dry. She turned back to the wall. Making her way up the hillside, she found a disused gate a short way ahead of her. Kassandra wasn't surprised to discover that it was both open and gave out onto the end of Potter's Field. While she was obviously going the way her mother wanted, she was a bit unsure of what the specter might expect of her. For the moment, she could only follow.

The lantern's light fell onto a hole excavated among a myriad of poorly dug graves, the mounds casting shadows that stretched out into the surrounding darkness. Lehvoi struggled at the pit's edge pulling something up from the depths. When he turned, the revelation of his visage gave truth to her prior vision. A strange and bizarre contraption covered his entire head. Fronted with a glass visor and sprouting tubes and cylinders, Kassandra recognized the monster from her dream. Always the germaphobe, Lehvoi must be protecting himself from the miasma of the shallow graves. As disturbing as his appearance was, it was nothing compared to his burden, the extended arm of a disinterred corpse. He struggled with the body, pulling it from the ground. As Kassandra put her hand over her mouth, she watched him reach for the spade that was thrust upright into the soil. Steadying the body with a foot, Lehvoi swung the shovel down on the wrist of the corpse again and again. As he hacked at it the sounds echoed through the plot and turned her stomach. At last he let the shovel fall to one side and lifted the severed hand. Lehvoi's prize went into a burlap sack, which he then slung over his shoulder, promptly followed by the spade. With a halfhearted kick, he tumbled the corpse back into its desecrated grave.

Watching Lehvoi disappear further into the graveyard with his burden, Kassandra found herself unwilling to follow. What did she think she was doing? Discovering that her teacher was a ghoul who not only dug up the dead but also dismembered them. She was having inexplicable visions and was convinced she was seeing her dead mother. Considering all of that, she'd be lucky if she weren't taken away to the bedlam house. Abruptly, Kassandra realized that the figure in black stood only a few yards away, the empty cowl of the cape facing her. There was a reflection of gold as a spectral hand gestured Kassandra forward. She took a deep breath and stepped away from the shadows where she hid. Maybe it was about time she remembered that she wasn't here for herself. She wasn't sure why Anastasia had led her here, but Kassandra had never doubted her. She followed her mother's spirit down the hillside to the last mausoleum on the outskirts of the graveyard.

While it was built of fine white marble, the joins and frame of the building were warped, its surface covered in moss. The broken levee Kassandra saw off in the distance explained the swamp engulfing this end of the graveyard. Brackish water came right up the back of the sepulcher. Light from Lehvoi's lantern cast shadows in the doorway, while Anastasia's shade ignored the entrance, walking around the side of the mausoleum.

The structure was bigger than Kassandra originally realized and shaped like a cross. As she walked around the left-hand wing trying to avoid the dead leaves scattered here and there, Kassandra stifled a shiver. While the night was warm, the damp-ness of her shoes and knickers wicked away the heat. At the edge of the reeds lay the apex of the cross and the farthest point of the mausoleum. Lehvoi's light shone through the narrow, leaded glass windows as he moved about the inside of the structure. A rusty gate covered the rear entrance and while it was unlocked, it creaked ominously when Cassandra pulled on the bars.

She studied the situation, hoping to find another way inside. Anastasia's shade stood in the darkness just beyond the bars waiting patiently. Looking around, Kassandra found a high-backed bench on the far side of the small stoop that fronted the gate. If she was daring enough and clambered up onto the back of the stone bench, she could probably step across to the top hinge of the gate. From there she could straddle the gate and leap down. Perhaps she had been right to cut off the lower layer of her skirt. Kassandra made her decision. She took one step up onto the seat of the bench. From there it was another step up on to the back and then a stretch over to the hinge. The gate wobbled once before she could straddle it and she hung on swaying. When she looked back over her shoulder Kassandra was surprised to see that the swamp was only a pace away from the stoop. Something stirred the black waters. She quickly swung her leg over the top of the gate and hung there for a moment before letting go. Her landing was surprisingly quiet. Peering in the dark, she could just make out Anastasia's retreating back. *Onward then,* she thought and moved to follow.

The mausoleum was dusty and lit only by the stray light from Lehvoi's lantern. Kassandra slid forward, leaning against the wall, her eyes straining through the half-light, searching for her mentor. As she moved, she realized that the floor of the building tipped at an angle down toward the back door. Strange scratching sounds came from all directions, echoing through the chamber. Pressed flush against the wall, she nearly stumbled into the alcove that opened ahead of her. When Lehvoi's lantern flashed about, she took advantage of the space, flattening herself against a rack of candles there. However, her mentor wasn't searching for the source of the sound, but rather placing the lantern on a large marble altar that dominated the center of the tomb.

In the flickering light, Kassandra made an effort to understand what she was seeing. While she couldn't explain its presence, she did recognize the large, glass static jar that sat next to the lantern. Thick wiring rose from its top and spread out like ivy run amuck, tacked to the ceiling with bent nails and running to every corner of the mausoleum. Lehvoi pulled off his mask and set it down next to the jar. He ran a hand though his hair, making it stick up in sweaty spikes. He mopped his brow with one of his ever-present handkerchiefs as he turned to inspect one of the various wooden installations emplaced along the stone walls.

Kassandra spared a moment to consider the writing stands set against the wall with rolls of paper descending into baskets at the base of each one. *What were they doing in a mausoleum?* The truly bizarre part was the half-decayed hands that gripped pens and scrawled on the paper. Each hand was attached to one of the cables that ran from the static jar. It came to her suddenly that the experiment from earlier with the frog bore a distinct

similarity to the arcane constructs that filled the central space of the mausoleum. As the sound changed, she became aware that several of the hands had stopped their work, put down their pens, and now pointed to her hiding place with accusing fingers. When Lehvoi lifted the lantern, Kassandra stepped forward, her right hand sliding inside her jacket to clasp the butt of one the pistols.

Shock caused her mentor to draw a sharp breath, but the disruption was only momentary.

"It is a bit overwhelming at first sight, isn't it, Kassandra?" Lehvoi asked clearly striving for the same tone he often used while teaching. Without waiting for her answer, he continued, "In the light of our earlier experiment you can see how deceased flesh can be made to react, but what most miss is the connection between the spirit of the departed and this reaction. Here I merely provide the opportunity and the shades then communicate across the gap of life and death itself."

"But why would they write anything at all?" asked Kassandra.

"Because the spirits know they are dead and this is the only way they can still communicate. At first they may be distracted and confused, perhaps even recalcitrant, but inevitably they all come around. All of the spirits that I have brought here have some precious gift of knowledge that can't be lost at any price."

"You can dress it up however you like, Lehvoi, but you are still a grave robber and a tomb desecrator. These people were laid to rest. They should have stayed that way, despite whatever they might know."

Lehvoi took a step closer. Kassandra strode forward to stand opposite him, placing the large static jar between them. As he slid to the left, she took another step to the right, maintaining their distance. "But what if the dead know something that would save lives, Kassandra? What if our enemies could tell us their secrets even after they'd fallen?"

She looked down a moment at the ream of paper that fell into the nearby basket as the hand mounted above it scribbled fiercely. In her peripheral vision, she saw Lehvoi take another two steps. She slid farther around, now on the complete opposite side from which she'd started.

"Can't you see, Kassandra, that questioning the dead is the only answer? The departed don't develop a conscience, don't become obstinate, and don't decide to lie. The dead have no choice."

"Perhaps they should." With that she produced her pistol and prayed he couldn't tell how badly her hands shook.

"Whatever are you going to do with that?" he asked with a sigh and crossed his arms over his chest, glaring at her.

It was a small movement, but it revealed something that she had missed. From where she'd entered the room, she couldn't see the hand in question and its pedestal. Only after moving around the perimeter and after Lehvoi took that last step was it visible. In the shifting lantern light an all-too-familiar ring shone on its finger.

Following her gaze, Lehvoi turned. "Now, Kassandra, you must understand that your mother was the most brilliant woman that I ever had the privilege of meeting. There was so much that she knew and never had the chance to pass along, that—" Lehvoi stopped, his eyes darting about and his mouth hanging open.

Her pistol was raised now and her grip steady, but Kassandra wasn't aiming at Lehvoi anymore. When she pulled the trigger, the blast shoved her back. The noise was swiftly followed by the explosion of the static jar, which blew the lantern across the room. Throwing an arm over her face she stumbled back as shards of glass flew about the chamber. Acid came pouring off of the upraised pedestal in the tomb's center. Kassandra backpedaled away from the smoking liquid as it splashed onto the containers of papers. Sparks shot from all of the connecting wires and started spontaneous fires, along with the blazing oil from the lamp. Across the flames, she watched Lehvoi turn and run for the rear exit, the draining acid pouring after him. Cautiously making her way around the edge of the room, Kassandra approached the wooden stand that held her mother's hand. She carefully extricated the desiccated remains, clutching them to her chest. Then, much as her mentor had, she turned and ran in the opposite direction, dodging fire and smoke.

Heaving in deep breaths, Kassandra leaned against the doorway of the mausoleum. The interior was lit with a hellish light as the contents continued to burn. Tucking her mother's hand into one of the large pockets in her jacket, she turned and determinedly set off after her erstwhile teacher.

When Kassandra reached the rear of the building she heard a disturbance in the nearby swamp. There, in the weak moonlight, she saw something thrashing amongst the reeds. Waving scaled lengths flailed about, reminiscent of her vision. Recognition came to her slowly. Those were alligator tails. The large reptiles roiled about in the water in a frenzy. A moment later, looking up at the open gate and the short path to the water below the mausoleum, it occurred to Kassandra that Lehvoi had met his end. Nauseated, she turned away and stumbled back to the front of the tomb.

Sitting on the steps leading up to the front of the mausoleum, Kassandra drew forth her mother's hand. She gently worked off the ring and clutching it hard in her own fingers until her breathing slowed. Lehvoi's shovel still leaned against the open gate. Kassandra supposed she ought to bury her mother's hand at her gravesite. She also realized that she now would need another teacher. Finally, she admitted to herself, she would have to come to terms with this new and perhaps dangerous gift that she had. Slowly, she noticed Anastasia's shade standing before her. The figure in the cloak leaned forward until Kassandra felt the faintest brush of lips on her forehead. When she looked up again her mother was gone. Perhaps her disappearance should have saddened Kassandra, but she suspect that Anastasia would always watch over her in some fashion. Turning the ring over, Kassandra slid it onto her finger. She wasn't the least bit surprised to discover that it fit perfectly.

BEYOND THE FAMILIAR

"THE DEPARTED HAVE BETTER THINGS TO DO THAN TALK TO YOU."

Kassandra met that statement from Madam Foss with a canted eyebrow.

"Look at me like that all you want, girl, but it's still the truth." The old medium tipped her teacup back and drank down the last dregs as Kassandra waited for her to continue. "It may sound absurd, but the dead don't always have an interest in the price of butter. They've moved on. They've joined the grand choir. They've earned their reward. They've other concerns."

Kassandra couldn't help but notice that as Madam Foss delivered her last comment her eyes drifted off to the right and she lifted the cup for another sip only to find she'd already emptied it. Kassandra enjoyed her time with her new mentor, surrounded by the scents of old book leather and candle wax, which made her feel at home. However, she often found that what Madam Foss avoided was as important as that which she relayed. Kassandra's father was the one who'd set up this apprenticeship, rather to her amazement. He'd told her that despite whatever he felt, it appeared she was taking after her mother's spiritual prowess, and the least he could do was introduce her to someone who could keep her safe.

Because it was expected of her, she asked, "Well, Madam Foss, how does one engage with the departed? My former teacher had the poor taste to rob graves, then force the spirits to speak."

Madam Foss's dark, wrinkled visage puckered up even farther, as if she'd been offered something scraped off of the road outside. "You and I will be avoiding any such wrongdoing. What we do is like a tool. You can build a house with it or lash about doing all sorts of damage. Such behavior has the potential of not only hurting others, but also yourself." With that, one of her brown fingers shot out and dug into Kassandra's chest. "You will be better than that wretch."

Leaning away, seemingly so she could reach for her tea while conveniently putting herself out of range of that finger, Kassandra considered her mentor. Madam Foss kept her hand outstretched for a moment longer and then settled back into her own chair. "We speak to the dead through intermediaries. There are those that are just as restless in death as they were in life. They can find the spirits we need to speak to and if those are unwilling to speak, the intermediaries can carry messages."

"They are familiars," Kassandra said suddenly, pleased with herself at the realization.

The chair creaked as Madam Foss lunged toward her once again, finger pointed, and then thought better of the action. She clutched her hands together, staring at Kassandra. "I keep forgetting that you are so much older than most who are brought to me." She shook her head, the gray curls swaying under her bonnet. "You like to think for yourself instead of listening like a younger apprentice would. Girl, if you say 'familiar' to anyone else, they'll be crying witchcraft in no time at all. What we do has nothing to do with the darkness we were discussing before. Perhaps spirits do become familiar and perhaps that's why they take such a name, but the common man knows that term only as evil. We speak to *intermediaries*, and to intermediaries only. We are mediums. The dead speak to us and we speak for them. That's all that matters. When someone decides they know better than we do, that's when words like 'evil' and 'witch' get tossed about. That's when they start gathering tinder."

She considered Kassandra for a moment longer, her dark eyes squinting as if she could see inside her charge. Then the passage of a dirigible droning by overhead broke her focus. She stood up suddenly and gestured for Kassandra to follow her. Setting aside her teacup, Kassandra brushed the front of her brown dress down and then stepped after her mentor as she crossed the sitting room and walked through the foyer.

A large staircase rose into the dimness of the upper level, dividing the house. Past it were a pair of large wooden doors. Kassandra had spent most of her time in the sitting room and the kitchen during her visits. They hadn't ventured beyond that until now. Madam Foss pulled out a large brass key, unlocked the doors, and then threw them wide. Dark curtains covered the windows in what appeared to be a converted dining room. Wooden chairs with caned bottoms had been spread around the perimeter, and a rich rug covered the floor. But what drew Kassandra's attention was the table at the center.

It was circular and draped in deep red velvet. A wooden disk lay on top, only slightly smaller in diameter. At its center was a hole through which braided copper wires rose from inside the table to latch on to the Jacob's Ladder that climbed halfway to the ceiling. Copper threads chased across the wooden circle in strange patterns and two brass handgrips were mounted close enough for easy use. A leather-backed chair was pushed up to the table in front of the grips.

Madam Foss pulled back the chair and said to Kassandra, "Sit."

Before, they'd merely been conversing. The tone that the medium took with her now was one that dropped Kassandra into the chair before she even considered rebelling. Instinctively, she reached out for the grips. They were so cold to her touch that she almost pulled away, but a sharp glance from Madam Foss made her keep her hands in place. The older woman reached down and turned a large crank that was just visible under the edge of the tablecloth. As she did so, a crackle snapped through the air and a flicker of static flew up the Jacob's Ladder, then another and another until visible arcs ascended toward the top and dissipated into the surrounding air. The copper wiring on the tabletop danced with fat blue sparks until the current hit Kassandra, shooting her hair out in all directions. Her red curls unfurled like a corona about her.

"Now you know why I wear a bonnet," came Madam Foss's dry comment.

But Kassandra scarcely paid attention. Her skin, her pores, her mouth, her eyes, her ears—every exit from her wept thin, translucent streams. Not water. Ectoplasm. Madam Foss had called it the insulation between worlds at one point. There it was, real as real could be, right before Kassandra. Gradually, the silver substance collected in a sphere over the table. When Kassandra looked down at the design in copper with its circles about the handgrips, she realized that it was designed to help keep the ectoplasm contained. The Jacob's Ladder overhead bled off just the right amount of static to keep the circuit she completed safe. More and more ectoplasm poured from her until the sphere swelled to twice the size of her head. She looked at it closely and discovered that it was spinning ever so slightly. Instinctively, she lunged forward out of the chair, and without a thought to Madam Foss's concerns plunged her head into the silver mass.

At first she didn't notice anything. It was almost as if her eyes were adjusting to a dark room. She definitely wasn't sitting at the table any longer. There came a faint sound that might be footsteps and a light breeze blew across her face. Gradually, she realized that she was looking down what she could only describe as a path. It was so straight and long that perspective vanished into the distance. She could see a little of what looked like woods to either side but couldn't actually move her point of view. It was as if her head weren't with her any longer, only her eyes. There were shapes and shadows ahead of her, however they were so far down the path they were more like suggestions or imperfections in the overall pattern. Then one of the shadows off to the side grew darker and became more defined. It stepped onto the path and crossed it quickly. Briefly, it hesitated. For the tiniest part of an instant, Kassandra had the impression of a dark cloaked form turning to stare at her before it faded into the other side.

The last time Kassandra had seen the shade of her mother, Anastasia, she'd worn a dark cloak. If there was any spirit she wished to speak to most it was certainly her. If Mother were to become her familiar spirit...pardon...her *intermediary*, it would be almost perfect. But the figure was gone. The path faded as Madam Foss's iron grip pulled her forcibly back into the chair and thus the mortal realm.

As Kassandra sat there gasping, her hands torn from the brass grips, Madam Foss considered her, hands akimbo. "Should've known you were going to do that. From now on, you head-strong girl, you listen to me, if you plan on staying on. The other side doesn't take kindly to intruders. There are things that keep us out. That's the important part. We *talk* to the other side. You don't get to visit unless you're planning on staying. Now you just sit back and I'll get you another cup of tea. Your heart's gonna race and be out of rhythm for a little and it's likely you'll have trouble catching your breath. You're young, so you'll do fine, but it'll hurt."

With that she reached underneath, pulled the handle she'd cranked into place against the underside of the table. As the apparatus threw out a few stray sparks, she patted Kassandra on the shoulder and wandered off after the tea.

While Kassandra sat there blinking, black spots chased across her vision as her heart thumped away like a swallow trapped in a chimney. She knew she would have a few moments to herself while Madam Foss fiddled away with the new auto-brewer that she'd bought to make her tea. Her mind was racing. Kassandra had seen what she would dare say was heaven. Well, she'd seen the other side, anyway.

It wasn't anything like she'd expected.

✝

In the weeks that followed, Kassandra continued to take a carriage across town from her father's home to call upon Madam Foss. Their relationship, however, had definitely changed. In short, Kassandra's task was to observe everything. While she hadn't been invited to sit at the table again, she found herself instead introduced as Madam Foss's assistant and was called upon to help the medium with her clientele. She took coats, made tea, and seated herself demurely behind Madam Foss while the woman asked questions of the departed. She noted, that while Madam Foss did the talking, the strange apparitions, which appeared over the table, had no voices. It didn't take her long to realize that Madam Foss was in fact reading the lips of her spirit guests. Kassandra soon began to learn the art herself.

One morning, she'd stolen into the sitting room to discover what her mentor had been looking at during their initial meeting. The bookshelf across from where she'd sat had a conspicuously empty spot. Reaching into the void, she'd found a small daguerreotype image. In the scratchy image a small ebony-faced child with heavy brows and a long nose held a cicada in their hands. The likeness reminded her of Madam Foss and the black curly hair could easily have turned gray. Kassandra carefully replaced the picture, brushing the dust back into place.

Two days later, while Madam Foss was cursing at her automated tea brewer, Kassandra slipped into the table room. She noticed that all of the chairs in the "working room," as Madam Foss called it, were attached to the floor and the various knick-knacks were affixed to the surfaces they rested upon. She'd felt the odd lightness produced by opening the way with ectoplasm and imagined things might become chaotic if not controlled. She'd taken an unsupervised moment to examine the table further and found the name Emond Ressex engraved on the wooden panel where the crank fitted in. Kassandra had heard of his reputation as a spiritualist and artificer.

After watching several sessions, it was obvious to Kassandra that when she'd sat at the table that first time, she'd merely begun the process of contacting the other side. Once Madam Foss had the requisite amount of ectoplasm collected, she would call out seeking an intermediary. Someone she referred to as Jasper often answered her. A caricature of a vaguely familiar face would then form on the surface of the ectoplasmic sphere. His answers were given by the motion of his lips without the evidence of any sound.

Madam Foss's intermediary appeared well informed. After a short wait, he told an elderly man that his wife had sold off her jewels before she passed away and where she'd hid the money. Another was informed that the property line that he believed was incorrectly drawn was accurate, however there was no way to prove it. A loved one was assured that their lost child was happy. The woman in black was told that her husband was in fact not dead but had run away.

Kassandra found herself admiring Madam Foss's ability to deal with all of these pronouncements. As far as Kassandra could tell, Madam Foss hadn't lied to any of them. She hadn't made them all happy either, but in the end they'd all paid her. Kassandra watched them as they'd left and noticed something different about each one. Something was lighter in their step; there was an absence of tension in their expressions or less of a slump to their shoulders. In each case the person who'd passed beyond—or had run off—left their supplicant with a need for closure. Madam Foss had given them that. It didn't matter whether they left in their carriage, steam-powered auto, or simply walked, each left as though a weight were lifted from them. It occurred to Kassandra that this ability was one she admired.

As much as she watched and learned, it wasn't enough. She desperately wanted to call for the ectoplasm once again and seek out the dark-cloaked figure she'd seen in the way between the worlds of the living and the dead. The reoccurring image in her imagination made her want to try something reckless, only Madam Foss had shown herself to be very observant and Kassandra was certain she would know if her student had used the table.

One afternoon, after a long session with an attorney seeking information about one of his less savory clients, Madam Foss sighed heavily and put a hand to her forehead. "I feel a fever coming on. Child, could you make me a cup of tea? I believe perhaps I should rest for the remainder of the day."

Kassandra did as her mentor asked, choosing the chamomile in the hope that it might make Madam Foss feel better. After a few sips, the old woman leaned back in her chair with a sigh. "I don't think I am up to dealing with the remaining appointment I have today. Can you be a dear and stay on to let them know that I won't be available? If you can, please reschedule them." She gestured offhandedly at the ledger clipped to the table behind her. "It won't be but an hour. Then you can go home." Then she pulled herself up to her feet unsteadily. Kassandra came to her side and helped her to the foot of the stairs. As she turned to ascend them, the old woman's hand clamped onto Kassandra's wrist. "I can trust you to take care of this, can't I?"

"Of course," Kassandra said, "It's no trouble at all." She watched the old woman make her way up the stairs and then went to recover the cup with its remaining tea.

Once she was in the working room again, Kassandra turned and faced the table. It would be so easy to sit down, but to do so would violate Madam Foss's trust. She tamped down the temptation and turned for the tea. It wasn't where she expected it. Instead the cup sat on the same table as the ledger. Shaking her head, she grasped the cup and found it oddly cold. Something moved on the edge of her vision and she turned quickly to find herself staring at her own image in the large mirror on the wall there. She was definitely nervous being left alone in the working room and it was starting to play on her nerves. Kassandra shook her head to clear her thoughts and started back to the kitchen. Tired herself, her feet shuffled across the carpet. She stared down at the teacup trying to martial her thoughts. Once again she felt that strange sense of being observed. But this time when she looked back to the mirror, her image had changed. Silver covered her lips and spun in wisps down her chin. Ectoplasm.

She rushed over to the mirror in fascination. As she did so more ectoplasm flowed from her. Only then did she look down at her feet and realize why. Static. She'd been rushing across the carpet and building up a static charge. Somehow this, like the charge of the table, brought on an ectoplasmic discharge. The tea cup in her hand forgotten, she leaned closer. The ectoplasm didn't flow like water. It was oddly wispy, almost like spider silk. A trickle came from her ears and nose as well as from her eyes. When she ran a hand over her face it clung unevenly to her fingers. That was when she noticed the first strands flowing from her to the mirror.

As she opened her mouth, a gush of silvery filaments splashed onto the glass in front of her. Gradually, the ectoplasm spread over the entirety of the surface. Webbings of light and shadow laced the distorted reflection. A frisson of panic ran through her. What had she done? And how could she undo it? A finger drawn across her lips assured her that no more ectoplasm gathered there. Perhaps it was time to confess to Madam Foss.

As much as she was loath to admit it, Kassandra was definitely out of her depth.

She strode across the carpet, careful to lift her feet. At the doorway, she hesitated. When she turned back to look at the mirror, she watched in amazement as a black-clad figure swept through the opening as though it were a window. Her fingers spasmed and the teacup fell to shatter across the floor. In that second, the specter dissolved into a mass of black mist that flew up to the ceiling. It clung there roiling like a black thundercloud and then shot out of the room. Kassandra followed it through the doorway.

Sliding across the tiled floor, she scrambled for the staircase seeking Madam Foss. As her foot struck the first riser, something crunched beneath her shoe. She grasped the banister to steady herself and felt things crackling and falling to pieces under her hand. A light brown object swung in front of her view. It caught in her hair as it fell over her face. She pulled it out and came to a halt staring at the cicada skin with a strand of her red hair still caught in its claws. When she turned around, she brushed aside more and more of the casings. They covered the stairway underfoot and clung to the threads of her brown tweed dress. As her head turned she felt more of them caught in her hair, spilling down her back and her blouse. The experience was so unexpected, she briefly forgot about the apparition she ran from. That was when she heard the humming above her, echoing in the stairwell.

It was a rustling sound, like leaves, but it also had a strange note to it reminiscent of a dynamo as it swelled and ebbed. When they began to sing, Kassandra knew what she was facing. The reason she could not see the lights in the upper hall was because it was filled with an enormous mass of cicadas. A sheer wall of glistening black carapaces, flickering veined wings, and tiny red eyes. It rippled as the insects clambered over one another in a constant twitching dance. Then the center of the mass pushed outward toward her. Starting at the top of the stairs, a shape began to emerge, coalescing from the horde of cicadas. Clutching at the banister, she saw the cloaked figure from the mirror emerge from the wall of insects, its form made up of the same clicking accumulation. She was gasping now, heart racing.

As she retreated, it stepped forward, the rest of the cicadas dropping from its shoulders like an obscene cape.

Kassandra felt her foot strike the tiled floor of the foyer. Was this the same spirit she had seen during her trip under the ectoplasm? The one she'd thought was her mother? She reached down and pulled off her mother's gold ring on her right hand, holding it before her. The whirring mass of cicadas continued to block her path. It had not reacted to the ring. Did that perhaps mean this wasn't her mother's shade, but rather something that had mimicked her to gain Kassandra's trust? Sucking in a breath, she stepped forward and in sync with her, the cicada shade stepped down the staircase. The shroud of insects parted to reveal its face, a mask of silver. The ectoplasm limned it in fine relief bringing out the long nose and heavy brows of a young man.

She understood now, this was a test. She might have convinced Madam Foss that she was worthy of her apprenticeship, but had she convinced the spirits? The features she'd seen covered in ectoplasm snapped into place in her memory. The picture. What if it was a relative...a brother...a nephew...a *son*...? One who had died. A spirit that would be eager to come when she called. Add fifteen years and the child in the picture could well have grown into the form before her.

"Jasper," Kassandra said on a taut breath.

The cicadas shifted uneasily.

Placing her empty hands out in front of her, palms up, Kassandra said, "Jasper, your mother believes that I have potential. I hope that you do as well."

The mass of insects continued down the stairs step by step until it stood before her. Gradually, the cicadas parted until the rest of the silvery form came to light underneath their bodies. Its hand reached out and a sharp finger poked her once above her heart in a very familiar gesture. Then it walked past her, turning toward the working room. The long cape of cicadas swept the floor as it passed through the doorway. Everywhere the insects touched, the shells that littered the ground vanished in silvery bubbles.

When she was finally able to breathe, she saw the cloud of cicadas stripped away from Jasper's ethereal form launch itself through the ectoplasm-hazed surface of the mirror. Jasper turned toward her and beckoned. Steeling her courage, she approached the spirit. When she stood before him, Jasper reached for her. Kassandra did her best not to flinch away. The silvery hands covered her face like a mask blocking out all light and Kassandra felt a water-like chill coat her skin. When at last something impinged on her senses, she once again found herself looking at the same strange path as when she'd thrust her head into the ectoplasm sphere.

She could feel Jasper beside her. His hands touched her face again, turning her. Now she could see that beyond the path and the stands of white-barked birch trees, rose towers and walls of alabaster. Open doorways, porticos, and gates led into the buildings. From everywhere came the ringing sounds of hammers and a white dust hung in the air. She wanted to speak, but found that here *she* had no voice. In a reversal of fortune it was Jasper who read her lips to answer her questions.

"No, you can't hear the choir. It is not for mortal ears. But what you can hear is the work."

His fingers lingered on her lips, drawing forth more questions. "What do we do? Why, we expand the mansion within the pearly gates. There are always more dead. Some imagine that the afterlife is nothing but the absolute in pleasure. How long at any given time have you truly been completely happy? And how long have you stayed that way? We're human. We don't know how to do that. Instead some of us find that the truest reward is to have a purpose. A purpose even like mine, protecting my mother and aiding her. There are as many purposes as there are the living and the passed on. It could be that even *you*, Kassandra, have a purpose."

That was when she felt them. The others lurking among the doorways, just out of sight. Waiting, waiting for her. The voices who would gladly answer when she called. She bowed her head. Then Jasper turned her once more. Pointing her back toward the light of the familiar. Nudging her toward life. But before she returned, Jasper had one last comment, "Your mother has a purpose as well. She has, however, realized that being close to you could draw dangerous attention. So she will be there for you, Kassandra, but it will be from a distance." With that,

Jasper pushed her back through the portal to the mortal realm. When she opened her eyes, Madam Foss stood framed in the doorway of the working room.

She nodded approvingly at Kassandra. "You have a lot of work ahead of you, girl, but my son is a good judge of character. You will do just fine." As she turned away, she threw over her shoulder, "If you listen to me that is."

Fox Chase

Kassandra looked up from the body in front of her to the man who'd just stepped into the small clearing. He tipped his head to one side, right hand coming to rest on the butt of the pistol holstered on his hip.

"Well!" he remarked as he considered the scene before him.

Standing up and straightening her riding skirt, Kassandra reached for the crop she'd tucked into her boot after dismounting. If he made a move for the gun, she'd only have one chance. In the golden light, preceding sunset, Kassandra recognized the other as one of the men from the fox hunting party. While accoutered in the traditional reds of the hunt and wearing a riding hat, he did not quite fit in with the others. In his single-word exclamation she'd caught enough of an accent to identify him as German. Then she placed him, she'd seen him in Roderic's party, an observant shadow rather than a politicking hanger-on. Dropping his hand from the pistol, he reached up, pulled off his hat, and gave her a brief bow. "Manfred Bremstrung at your service, madam."

Kassandra offered her hand. "Madam Kassandra Leyden." She couldn't help but notice that his eyes did a cursory search of her small fingers as he clasped them. "No, I didn't kill him, before you ask," she said taking her hand back. His eyes had sought a ring and after that a certain questioning look entered his gaze. "And I am not that sort of madam, rather an intermediary with the departed. Let's just say if folk didn't have the misfortune to die, I wouldn't have much of a business."

"Well, I for one would rather we continued our conversation while I am still animate. As for killing the gentleman in question, if you had managed it, I would say you were quite skilled, given the severing of the jugular and the spray of blood about the laurels here. Also down here I can see a series of slashes on the fellow's jodhpurs where he was hamstrung. Interestingly, the neck wound seems to be a series of cuts rather than a single blow." Bremstrung dropped to a knee away from the blood.

Kassandra leaned closer, pushing her ringlets of red hair back from her face. "Almost looks like a bite, since there are two series of cuts above and below."

"Indeed, madam, well spotted, but what sort of beast might do this?"

A low moan came from the far side of the clearing. Pulling his pistol, Bremstrung moved from the light into the shadows and crept toward the sound. Pushing aside laurel branches, he gave a gasp and tossing aside his weapon, reached into the bushes to reveal another fox hunter dressed in red and white—but in this case red stained his white jodhpurs and boots as well.

Kassandra immediately recognized his face as she stepped over the dead man to aid Bremstrung. *What had attacked Roderic, the nephew of His Majesty King Edward XXIII, and the other hunter?* she wondered as she tore the bottom from her petticoat and offered the material to Bremstrung.

He accepted it and whistled a shrill note, calling his horse into the clearing. The well-trained roan, trailing its reins, walked up to them. Bremstrung pulled down the canteen that hung from the back of his saddle, offering it to Roderic. After the young man choked down a few mouthfuls, Bremstrung used the remainder to clean off the wound on the front of Roderic's shin and then, using Kassandra's contribution, bandaged it up.

Roderic's eyes flickered open showing just whites. "F-f-fox, bloody shining fox," he murmured. Then he slid forward to become a limp burden in Bremstrung's arms.

Kassandra brushed back Roderic's hair from his forehead revealing the reddish swelling there. "Well that explains that. Must have hit his head when he was pitched from his horse." Something caught her eye and she reached down to Roderic's boot to pick up a shiny clump of fur. It was unlike anything she'd ever seen. She could swear that it was made strands of copper. Showing it to Bremstrung, she stated, "I can't explain this, however."

Giving it a cursory glance, Bremstrung shook his head. "Does not matter. Our priority has to be getting His Lordship to safety." Turning his gaze to her, he met her eyes. "In case you have not guessed, I am here to watch over Roderic."

"Makes sense, a German would be someone I wouldn't immediately suspect. I suppose the unfortunate fellow who's lying behind us was Roderic's public guard? I imagined that you were something more from your actions, as well as your horse. It's a well-trained animal that doesn't spook at the smell of blood and responds to signals like that."

"Well, Madam Kassandra, you are not exactly ordinary yourself, having a history of helping out the constabulary using metaphysical means that most would scoff at. You see I have made myself familiar with all of the participants here, as part of my duty. But enough of that, we were making for Fox Chase hunting lodge when all of this misfortune started. Something went crashing through the undergrowth and I went off to investigate. That's when I heard someone cry out and returned to find you standing over Walter." Bremstrung spared a brief glance at the sky overhead. "The light is waning. Best we were off."

As she put a toe into the stirrup and vaulted up onto her horse, she felt a brief moment of frustration. She wasn't really here to hunt fox; instead she was hunting a man, one Emond Ressex. While her father had sent her off on this venture in hopes of catching the eye of some young noble, in typical fashion she'd subverted the enterprise to her own ends. Kassandra was intent on meeting Ressex, since he was one of the few spiritualists who had achieved public acceptance, as well as Royal approval. The man was also an adept artificer and that made him much more interesting than any potential matrimonial match. But so far she hadn't seen him. Of course, an interruption such as his lordship and an unexpected body certainly had set things awry.

Bremstrung turned to settle Roderic onto the saddle of his horse, avoiding his rifle in its side holster. Wondering at the strange arrangement of lenses fitted to the top of the weapon, Kassandra took the moment to place the unusual piece of fur in the front pocket of her riding vest. She caught her horse's reins and led the mare to join Bremstrung. There was a hint of burning wood, which caught her attention. "Smells like smoke in this direction," she said pointing at a small game path.

"*Wunderbahr*," replied Bremstrung as he swung up into the saddle behind Roderic, one hand on the reins, the other steadying his charge. "It is good we have your nose. My poor sense of smell could never have solved that mystery."

"What about this one though, Master Bremstrung, where are these men's horses?"

"Run off perhaps?"

"Hopefully just that."

Bremstrung turned to her before starting down the path. "What? I thought we'd determined this was an animal attack?"

"Let's just say that my job communicating with the dearly departed makes me tend to closely regard the unusual. But you are right; no matter what the situation, we are better off at the lodge. What was Roderic's guard's name?"

"Walter Pelton."

Looking back at the body, she whispered, "Sleep now, Walter. You did not fail. Your charge is well." She wished she had more time but Bremstrung was keen to be off. Then something in the woods caught her eye. A flicker of reflected moonlight shone on a form amongst the trees. A long, white-tipped tail snapped above the ghostly beast's spine as every hair on its sleek body shimmered. Kassandra's second sight was also drawn to the otherworldly creature and for a second she could swear she saw the heads of three dogs wavering above it like a spectral Cerberus. In another instant it was gone. Considering Bremstrung's reaction to the fur she'd found, she brushed aside the thought of sharing her observation and urged her mare onward after him.

A short while later they emerged from the woods into the light streaming from the windows of Fox Chase lodge. As she dismounted to help Bremstrung with Roderic, Kassandra couldn't help but notice his sudden attention to the horses tied to the railing. "That's Roderic's bay," he said with a nod of his head. They shared a look. The missing horses had returned to the lodge. *What if this were more than an unexpected animal attack?*

She wondered briefly at why the horses were tied along the rail, until she glanced at the nearby stable. The moonlight shone into the open door enough to reveal the brass-worked body of a steam lorry. Of course, the blasted reason she had yet to meet Emond Ressex. Pulling Roderic's arm over her shoulder, she ruefully considered how her plan had gone awry.

Ressex and his assistant Saul must have arrived late for the hunt in the motorized vehicle. Magistrate Cornwell had ordered them to the lodge to ensure the hunting party was not interrupted. Kassandra had spent more time surveying the group of riders than following the hounds and in so doing ended up discovering the remains of poor Walter.

Bremstrung brought them to a halt before the door of the fieldstone lodge, resetting his rifle back onto his shoulder. "If I might impose, Madam, will you help me watch over Roderic until we can ascertain if anyone intends him harm?"

So much for my plans, thought Kassandra, but if she were looking for Royal approval there certainly were worse ways to achieve it than aiding Edward's nephew. "I've some small experience in nursing, so certainly I will help." She neglected to mention that most of that was caring for her drink-sodden father, but now was neither the time nor place.

As Bremstrung did an admirable job of fending off the attention their arrival produced, Kassandra's eyes swept the room. She swiftly identified Ressex and was gratified that the man gave her a small nod of his head. Perhaps all was not lost in her pursuit, then. Next to him, Ressex's protégé Saul gave her a sneer and turned back to poking at the fireplace where the flames cast a ruddy hue on his tweed vest and patched boots. *Did he believe she sought his place?* she wondered.

The magistrate pushed his way to the front using his substantial bulk and proceeded to blunder about with loud exclamations about Roderic's state. His wisp of a daughter, Caitlin, who was to be Kassandra's rooming companion, seemed to have descended into a state of vacuous shock. *If nothing else,* thought Kassandra, *at least I've been spared the fate of entertaining the girl.*

"We really should let Roderic retire for the evening to rest, sir," suggested Bremstrung.

"Of course, of course," blustered Cornwell, plowing a path through the concerned hunters and leading them up the stairway to the third floor. His bald pate reflected the passing candles as he came to a stop in front of the corner room.

"It would be best if we were not disturbed. Madam Leyden will be staying with us since she has some nursing experience," Bremstrung stated.

"But it is not seemly...and what of my daughter?"

"I suggest she lock her door, just as we will be doing here." Bremstrung pulled the heavy oak door closed with a snap. After they'd settled Roderic in the bed, Bremstrung made his way about the room looking over the walls. "So, notice anything suspicious when we brought Roderic in?" he asked pulling back the drapes on the window to reveal the stand of immense hemlocks that encircled the Fox Chase lodge.

Kassandra tucked Roderic's hand under the coverlet, satisfied that he was asleep. "No. There seemed to be genuine concern from everyone present, not to mention panic in Cornwell's case, of course. Something like this could ruin him instead of raise him up." For a moment she thought back to Saul's expression, but discounted it as jealousy because she'd sought out Ressex. Perhaps her letter campaign hadn't been successful due to his intervention. She brushed the thought aside, settling into a brocade-covered chair.

"In the morning, we will have to find a way to get Roderic out of here safely." Bremstrung settled into the chair on the other side of the bed. Pulling out a handkerchief, he began working over his pistol, cleaning its various workings. In the corner behind him rested the rifle with its strange series of lenses. When he'd finished, Bremstrung dropped the pistol in his lap. "Why not see if you can get any sleep? I will keep watch."

"Wake me later and I will spell you," Kassandra replied, easing further back into the chair.

"I will wake you, and we will discuss it."

She closed her eyes, smiling, certain he had no intention whatsoever of disturbing her sleep. The room dimmed as Bremstrung shuttered the lamp that sat on the dressing table and snuffed the candles in their sconces. Kassandra thought back to the strange vision she'd seen in the woods. What exactly did the three heads of the dogs mean? The more she thought about it there seemed to have been a driven look in their eyes. What also of the strange ghostly fox that shone as if polished?

Lying there dozing, Kassandra flinched awake at a scraping sound coming from the window. Sitting up, she had only a moment to notice Bremstrung coming to his feet when the glass of the window exploded into the room as something burst through the pane. In the dim half-light of the shuttered lamp, the lithe form of an otherworldly fox flew through the air to strike the end of the bed at the terminus of its leap. Kassandra hesitated a second, staring half in fear and half in wonder at the apparition before simply reacting. Reaching over, she grasped the bedding and hauled Roderic toward her until he slid onto the floor with a thump. The fox's sharp claws shredded the mattress until feathers flew, whirling about the room in the cold night breeze from the broken window. As Roderic tried to sit up, Kassandra scurried to his side and pulled him down. The fox's head swung toward them both with a strange mechanical whine.

A sharp click drew Kassandra's attention away from their attacker. Bremstrung stood beside the bed, his left knee resting on the mattress, pistol aimed at the animal. For a moment the tableau held. As feathers gently wafted down, the gun spoke with a sharp retort flinging the fox across the room into the wooden door. Cocking the hammer again, Bremstrung sent another bullet into the beast's innards. Suddenly, the room was full of singing bits of metal as the fox burst into pieces.

"What in God's name is happening?" asked Roderic into the sudden silence.

Ignoring the question, Bremstrung strode to the window and stared out into the night. "Damned thing leapt from that hemlock just out there." He reached out of the window and pulled the storm shutters closed across the gap in the broken glass.

Kassandra crawled across the floor to the still-twitching mass by the door. The jaws on the fox's copper head clacked open and shut spastically. Portions of beast's body were scattered about the room: steel bones, copper fur, and brass gears. Some of the internal bolts and springs had been driven into the walls from the force of their ejection. Its eyes flicked to her briefly and then wandered about the room until they found Roderic. The last functioning front paw scraped at the floor as the broken body tried to pull its way toward the shaking young man wrapped in blankets.

"I do not think so." Bremstrung's kick lofted the fox's remains into the air, sending it crashing into the wall near the dressing table. The lamp wobbled, sending shadows flickering about the room. Another spring burst loose, striking Bremstrung on the temple, cutting a runnel of blood that splashed into his blond hair.

Kassandra considered what she had seen. The beast had recognized Roderic—it had singled him out. She moved over to the now-quiescent remains and stirred them with a toe. A circle of dark metal slid out onto the floor. It was etched with a strange symbol and when she picked it up dark flecks of dried blood fell from the grooves. The image of a dog impinged once again on her second sight. The spectral creature stood right there before her, snapping madly, foam flying from its ghostly jaws. But its eyes, its eyes were again fastened on the prince. The spirit lunged at her because she stood between it and Roderic. The longer she held the light, thin disk, the colder it became. Her fingers found something round attached to the other side. *What is a button doing here*? she wondered.

Bremstrung held his handkerchief to his forehand after reloading the pistol. "It was an automaton? That makes no sense. I have seen automatons before. They are clunky and graceless. This thing moved like a real animal. A deadly animal."

"And it was fixated on Roderic," Kassandra stated, holding up the icy metal disk.

Bremstrung stared at it, his head moving slightly from side to side.

"You see it?" she asked bringing the disk closer.

"It is like a heat shimmer."

"It's the ghost of a dog—a trained killer. That's what gave the machine its grace. The fox skin is just the shell. Someone found a way to bind the spirit to this machine and gave it a purpose. Like any ghost, once it fulfils its purpose, it would go free."

When Kassandra flipped over the disk, Roderic leaned forward. "That's one of my buttons," he exclaimed.

"Well that's how it fixated on Roderic. It had something of his," mused Kassandra. She took the disk in her hands and began rubbing it back and forth between them, forcing the friction to warm it. But instead it grew colder with each motion. Finally, she brought the disk up and pressed it against her forehead. The intense chill made her gasp. With her second sight she had one brief glimpse of a hand wielding a knife against the throat of a struggling hound and then blood fell, spattering onto patched boots. Pulling the disk from her head she gave a gasp. She knew those boots. They belonged to Saul.

Kassandra reached out to catch Bremstrung's hand, holding him back. "It's Saul," she whispered. "The ghost remembers being killed by him." Then she clenched the disk in her hand and crushing its flimsy surface. The vaporous remnant of the dog's ghost disintegrated before her.

Bremstrung shifted his jaw to one side, seemingly considering the news before gesturing Roderic over to join them. "We are leaving and we are taking their vehicle to escape. It is no longer safe here for Roderic."

"Wouldn't the horses be faster?" asked Kassandra as Bremstrung reached back for his rifle.

"The horses do not have a door that locks," was his terse reply as he turned to the entrance of the room.

"Is no one going to tell me what on earth is going on?" asked Roderic standing behind them with his arms crossed.

Bremstrung turned and said, "No!" Then he relented and added, "Follow us and we have a good chance of saving your life. Otherwise, I cannot make any promises."

A hammering on the door made them all jump. Bremstrung pulled it open to reveal a red-faced Cornwell. He grasped the magistrate's lapels and pulled him within, shutting the door firmly behind him.

Cornwell's eyes darted about the room. "What on earth happened here?"

"It does not matter. Listen, to me, sir; we need to get Roderic to safety. To do that, we will need a distraction and you shall serve admirably. Magistrate, I need you to rouse the men below and tell them that you heard shots. You must tell them that you believe Roderic has been wounded. Once they discover that we are no longer in the room, keep them searching the lodge as long as possible. Can you do this?" Bremstrung asked, his hands on the magistrate's broad shoulders.

"Why, of course..." Cornwell's replied. Bremstrung cut off the rest of his reply, pushing the man ahead of him into the hallway.

A moment later they were rushing down the servants stairwell and out through the storm cellar doors into the night. The tall shapes of the hemlocks obscured the moonlight; the three of them stumbled in the darkness until Kassandra saw Bremstrung's outstretched hand happen upon the wall of the stable. He swiftly ushered them within. Kicking about in the straw, Kassandra found her way to the rear of the steam lorry. She snatched her hand back with a pained gasp. "We're fortunate. It appears they've only banked the coals, instead of emptying the pan. We should be able to get the steam going quickly."

"So, you know how to drive one of these vehicles? Why that's quite fascinating," nattered Roderic as he came to her side.

"How hard can it be?" she answered, placing a hand to his shoulder and shoving him toward Bremstrung. Taking the opportunity as it came, the German used the momentum to swing Roderic up into the backseat. He then clambered up to sit behind the steering wheel but hesitated. Kassandra turned back to the coal furnace and stirred the embers to life before tossing on more lumps. Walking around the front of vehicle, she joined Bremstrung in the carriage. "Well?" she asked.

"I will remind you that you are the one who made the comment about the difficulty of driving this contrivance."

"Really." Kassandra leaned forward and, after tapping at a gauge, she grasped a lever near Bremstrung's knee. Pushing the caliper at its top closed, she grinned broadly as the lorry lurched ahead. But her happiness was short lived as Saul stepped from the darkness with a shining fox at his side.

Bremstrung did not hesitate. He shoved the lever down and the lorry sped forward. He twisted the wheel and rode Saul down. A look of horror passed over the man's features and then the lorry bore him under with a sickening crunch. Kassandra watched the fox dance daintily to the side before turning to pursue them. Clearing the doorway of the stable, the vehicle made rapid progress toward the gate with the fox bounding along behind. Looking away from the roadway, Bremstrung shouted, "Rifle," over his shoulder at Roderic. Kassandra watched the young royal fumble with the large weapon. Bremstrung then turned to her and snapped, "Wheel."

She looked at him and then the wheel and said in a panicked voice, "You are mad."

Not giving her a choice, he let go of the steering device and reached for the rifle. Kassandra lunged for the wheel as Bremstrung's window slid down and he shoved the barrel out. Kassandra spared him only momentary glances as she struggled to keep the lorry in the ruts of the roadway. Fumbling with the lenses, he brought up the gun. Cresting high on the turn, the lorry jumped and Bremstrung cursed something long and complicated in German. "Keep it steady!" he growled, re-aiming. Looking back, Kassandra saw the fox gaining on the carriage. Then the rifle spoke, the interior of the lorry ringing with the sound. A blaze of copper lit by moonlight spun off into the woods, various parts of the automaton scattering across the roadway as the fox came to an abrupt stop.

Roderic turned to them with a grin. "Safe at last!"

Kassandra watched Bremstrung toss the rifle over his shoulder into Roderic's lap and reach to regain the wheel. She did not share Roderic's relief. There was something bothering her and now that she wasn't leaned half in Bremstrung's lap attempting to keep the lorry moving in a controlled fashion, she could spare some consideration. Why had she seen three heads over the first fox and only one on the remains of the broken one at the lodge? Perhaps she wasn't just seeing just the ghost of the dog, but rather a premonition. She drew in a deep breath in apprehension. "Lock the door and shut the window. Do it now!" In the moment's hesitation from both of the men, she heard a ripping sound as the leather top of the lorry parted and copper claws showed through.

Reaching over and pulling on the lever by Bremstrung's knee, Kassandra heard a blast of steam whistle through the exhaust pipes that jutted upward from the rear of the vehicle. A moment later Bremstrung stomped a pedal on the floor and the vehicle skidded to a stop. The mechanical fox rolled across the top of the lorry, then came to a stop hanging in front of the glass windscreen with one paw still caught in the rooftop. The jaws snapped at the window and the claws clattered across the glass.

Kassandra was somewhat surprised by the creature's behavior until she realized that the fox's eyes were covered in condensation from the blast of steam. "It can't see," she cried.

That was the only invitation Bremstrung needed. He stood partway up in the seat and pulled out his pistol. With his left arm he battered at the leather roof until it gave. Forcing his way out of the top, he leaned forward and rapped the pistol once on the windscreen. The head of the fox whipped around. Bremstrung shoved the barrel into the copper fur between its eyes and pulled the trigger. The bullet passed through the head and into the body as cogs, springs, and metal fur exploded into the night, pinging and bouncing across the front hood of the vehicle.

Kassandra sat back with a sigh. When she glanced over her shoulder, she found a shivering Roderic clutching the rifle. Bremstrung pulled himself back through the rent in the roof and sat down heavily. "That should be all of them," Kassandra offered sitting up a little straighter.

"Well that was plenty. I suppose we could go back to the lodge," Bremstrung said, brushing bits of copper fur from his coat.

"I, for one, am quite through with anything that has to do with foxes for a while," stated Roderic.

Kassandra found it the first sound piece of conversation that he'd offered. When Bremstrung looked at her, she nodded her head in the direction of the road. Without another word, he drove the vehicle into the night, the moonlight occasionally playing over his features as it pierced the shredded roof.

Sitting in her father's garden and considering her future, Kassandra's gaze lingered over the missive that had recently arrived for her. It bore no other marking than her name. When she unfolded its intricate design she discovered a few lines in a refined hand.

> *My Dear Madam Leyden,*
>
> *Many thanks for your efforts on behalf of my recent endeavors.*
> *Whilst the experiment was not a complete success, you were beneficial in determining its weaknesses.*
> *If you should ever require any future assistance, do not hesitate to seek me out.*
>
> *ER*

Of course...a master would not sully his fine boots while performing the unpleasant task of slaughtering the dogs to gain their ghosts. He would borrow his protégé's old and soiled ones. The letter fluttered from her suddenly lax fingers to land upon the ground.

DRINKING DOWN DEATH

"SHUT IT!" CONSTABLE COBHAM PECKWITH BROUGHT HIS TRUNCHEON around in an arc, making the iron door of the cell ring like a gong. The lady to his left jumped visibly. Cobham reached up and tugged at his hat briefly. "Sorry, ma'am. Wasn't my intent to startle you. These here get a bit odd now and then."

"Whatever do you mean?" Already she was stepping forward to the small barred window and stretching up to peer within.

Cobham was at a loss. He certainly wasn't going to lay hands on her, but these new addicts were unpredictable. He leaned forward and put a hand against the door very close to her cheek. "Best step back. They have this strange tendency to sing. Doesn't make a damn bit of sense, but if you get more than five of them together, then strange things start to happen. People start to pay too much attention to them."

Looking at his hand, with its rough skin and scars, and then turning her blue eyes to his, she stepped back. "The strange often seem to cluster together like grapes, Constable."

At that point Constable Whytburn barreled down the passageway bearing a huge book open before him. Whytburn's unkempt blond hair stuck out at all angles and his brass-framed, half-moon spectacles gave him a startling look like he'd escaped from a fairytale. The constable's other penchant for muttering under his breath as he walked certainly didn't help; however, the man was a veritable font of information in most cases. Whytburn plowed his way between them mumbling, "Glossolalia. Must be. No other explanation." He came to a stop after two steps and turned abruptly on his heel. "But why? Why would they all have glossolalia?" Cobham and his charge looked at each other, unsure if the question was actually addressed to them. They were interrupted by the rattling of a cylinder blundering its way through the steamline overhead carrying information vital to police business. In that moment of disruption, Whytburn had already turned yet again to plunge onward into the station house. Young Avery appeared next, gave them both a respectful nod, and charged after Whytburn calling his name.

"Terribly sorry about that. He isn't usually quite that rude," apologized Cobham.

"Quite a few officers about tonight. That is a little unusual, isn't it, Constable?"

"Well," Cobham stated, "The ambassador to the Southron Islands is in town to meet with the Islander delegation this week. Tonight he'll be at the opera house relaxing and we've stepped up our security." He broke off the conversation, unwilling to reveal any more. Instead Cobham turned to lead his guest further down the hallway. He stopped when he realized she wasn't following him.

"Glossolalia," she said quietly. She turned and faced the door to the cell again, tapping a forefinger to her lips, head cocked to one side.

"Ma'am, you did say that you wanted to make a statement."

"Yes. Sorry, just distracted, and I did warn you about how strange things tend to cluster, Constable."

Cobham hesitated a moment. He really had no time for those that were extraordinary. The ordinary kept him quite busy enough, stealing, knifing one another, and generally causing an endless amount of unrest in the streets of the port of Amphyra. The drunks and addicts of all sorts of unsavory substances he could handle, but this new drug was something else. No one had seen the narcotic, only found odd stoppered silver canisters. It was spreading rapidly though, like a sickness. His investigative instincts made him ask, "Do you know what he meant by that, ma'am?"

She turned her canny gaze to him and drew her lips up sharply. "We can't really go on like this, Constable. We need a proper introduction."

"Terribly sorry, ma'am, we seem to keep getting distracted. My name is Constable Cobham Peckwith."

"Pleased to meet you, Constable, I am Madam Kassandra Leyden. Perhaps we can retire to somewhere less public and discuss the missing persons I've come about? Do drop that eyebrow, Constable, the title 'Madam' does not refer to the employment you are guessing. I am a medium. Why am I always forced to correct people?" She rolled her eyes.

"Ah, certainly. My apologies. This way." Cobham started to turn and then stopped. "But you haven't really answered my question, have you? In order for us to proceed with a proper investigation, I will need you to be completely forthcoming."

"Well then, glossolalia is speaking in tongues—sometimes believed to be the language of the seraphim. And why would I possess such knowledge you might wonder? Well my employment is speaking to the dearly departed, who tend to have a firsthand experience with such things. In reality, I am here—" Kassandra hesitated, gathering her resolve, then she took a breath and continued, "Because all of the other practitioners of my art in Amphyra have vanished."

✟

Standing at the foot of the steps to the station house Cobham turned up the collar on his uniform. The steamlines crawling up the wall behind him branched out all through Amphyra. Moisture condensed on their exteriors and they shook as message cylinders shot through them. The winter breeze and fog rolling in off of the sea chilled him as he considered the scrawl in his battered journal. There were six names, the allegedly vanished spiritualists. He ought to just pick one to start with and get moving. There were footsteps and a clicking sound to his left. He turned to discover Madam Leyden standing there, her umbrella before her, hands resting on its gnarled wooden handle. Her feet were tight together and her back straight like a first-year recruit. She was so prim and proper; it took him aback. "Shall we?" she asked.

"Perhaps it would be best if you left this to me, ma'am."

"Given your reaction to my information, I think it best that I accompany you on your inquiries. You might even find my insights helpful." With that she spun on her heel and, lifting her umbrella, she pointed down the street. "This way."

Pursing his lips, Cobham fell in beside her on the left. The gaslights flickered in the breeze and the condensation from the vents of the subterranean steam lines hazed the air as they walked along the cobbles.

"You're grinding your teeth, Constable."

"Sorry, ma'am. Bad habit."

Kassandra pointed across the street. In the midst of their crossing, the illumination from the lighthouse speared out through the fog scattering reflections from the dirigible caravan droning by overhead. Cobham became aware of a sound that was nearly drowned out by the *whir* of the passing motors—a carriage, approaching at speed. He reached out and bodily swung Madam Kassandra around in front of him, pushing them both out of the avenue. She caught herself, using the umbrella to stay her momentum and provide support. Cobham, however, struck the wall and fell forward to his knees in the gutter.

The wide van swung through the narrow way, the breath of the horses clouding the air. Cobham had a brief impression of a pair of folded hands superimposed over a closed eye painted on the side of the van. The mist and fog around them swirled with the vehicle's passage. For a moment he thought he could perceive a form moving among the vapors. At his side, Kassandra leaned forward, peering into the darkness. She darted into the street and stooped to peer at the cobblestones.

Cobham pushed off the brick wall beside him until he regained his feet. Reaching back, he flattened the poster he'd knocked loose until it adhered to the wall once more. Briefly he noted the words '*FANTASTIC NEW INVENTION OF THE KENSINGTON AUDIBLE CYLINDROGRAPH TO BE SHOWCASED AT THE AMPHYRA OPERA HOUSE TO AMAZE ONE AND ALL*'.

"The Sisters of Perceptual Emotion. Wherever could they be going in such a rush?" asked Kassandra, leaning heavily on her umbrella.

Cobham replied, "They're off to the station house. We haven't been able to handle all of the cases of the Singers. The sisters take the victims in and treat them. We've only got so much room at the station house and the cases seem to grow by the hour."

"Constable, when did you find the first of these 'Singers' as you call them?"

"'Bout two weeks ago, last Tuesday, I would say."

"Interesting," was her response. "Change of plan, Constable, we'll be going this way now."

"Why not the first address?"

"One of my fellow practitioners of the spiritual arts has contacted me."

"What are you talking about?" asked Cobham, arms crossed over his chest.

"Look." She was pointed at the ground with the tip of her umbrella. There was something silvery lettered on the ground "CLXXV". "That would be Mandilla's address. She was no friend of mine, but I wouldn't wish this on anyone."

"Wish what?"

"Do keep up, Constable; if I've communicated with one of our missing spiritualists, given the nature of my profession—I am afraid she's dead."

"Well are you going to break down the door?"

"Ma'am, I am an officer of the law. I'm planning on knocking. If there's no one about, we'll consider other options."

"There's rapping at the gate out of the way. What next, Constable?"

Cobham looked at the narrow brick entryway. He walked to the nearby alley and looked up, considering the building. "We'll try around back. This seems to be all one home."

"Clever deduction, lead on."

The backdoor was open and Cobham stepped into the small mudroom. He listened briefly. There was every indication no one was at home. They made their way through the darkened house until they came to the main parlor. Kassandra's face shone in the light of a struck match as she lit the gas wall lamps. Cobham glanced about the open space, dominated by a large round table. Two brass grips rose above its strangely intagliated surface. The walls were hung with odd pictures. Streamers of light or glowing balls surrounded their subjects. There were all sorts of bric-a-brac. Some, like the stuffed fox head, were grisly in nature.

Kassandra propped her umbrella against the wall and pulled the most ornate chair to the table.

"Shouldn't you be looking for clues, Constable?"

"And what are you planning on doing?"

"I'm planning on talking to dearly departed Madam Mandilla, of course."

"Rubbish."

"This is my job. If you have no belief in the realms beyond the natural, humor me, for my life may depend on it."

Cobham met Kassandra's intense stare and found himself looking away and nodding. He really didn't want to invest any time at all in what he considered foolishness, but perhaps he could look about the home while she played at communing with the afterlife. He went to a small writing desk, pulled open the drawer, and turned over the papers inside with a finger. Hearing a gasp he turned back.

Kassandra leaned over the table, her hands grasping the brass grips as hints of St. Elmo's fire crawled about her wrists. "To meet the dead, I will travel part of the way to them. When we have our message, I may need you to bring me back. Ever done anything like that, Constable?"

Cobham shuffled his feet briefly and thought of the young man the watch had fished out of the bay two days before. How the doctor had pounded on the victim's back until the lad had coughed up a puddle of seawater. Meeting her eyes, he reddened slightly at the thought of performing the same deed on the lady before him. "Yes," he forced out, turning away once more.

"Remember, Constable, only when we have our message," she said sharply.

There was an abrupt crackling sound like a lightning strike. Cobham forced his attention back to the desk. In the far corner was a spike with a series of receipts impaled upon it. The name at the top looked familiar. He pulled it off and bent for a closer examination. As he did so, he realized everything on the table floated gently above its surface. The receipt almost slipped through his fingers and he swiftly tucked it into his vest. Stepping back involuntarily, he noted that all of the pictures in the room now hung in the air several inches out from the wall. Cobham spun slowly on his heel to face the spectacle of the divining table.

Kassandra still gripped the brass handles as witchlight and static flickered along her cheeks and through the mass of her hair, which stood on end. Now something slick coated her and oozed with a mirrored surface like mercury. Suddenly, everything came back to earth. The sound of shattering glass filled the room and Cobham stumbled realizing that even he had been floating.

He fell forward, hands coming to rest on the edge of the table. For a moment he felt the current rippling through him, making his muscles twitch. Then he staggered back, leaning against the writing desk, his feet crushing more pieces of glass strewn about the floor. Every bit of the shining fluid had leapt from the medium to hang in glistening droplets floating in the air about her. Cobham was assailed by the odor of rusting iron and the pungent stench of the docks. The arcane liquid in the room suddenly collapsed into a sphere that spun over the center of the table.

As he watched, features began to form on the globe of iridescent material. Hair formed waves in the quicksilver. Kassandra stared intently at the moving lips. Cobham realized he was holding his breath. Something bothered him. In amongst all of the strange odors there was something oddly sweet tinged with the tang of ozone. He'd smelled that before. Where had he smelled that? A loud thump ended his distraction—Kassandra's head had fallen forward onto the table and, from what he could see, she wasn't breathing.

Cobham worked his way around the table, cautious of its charge. As quick as he could, he hooked a foot through the legs of the chair and tipped her back into his arms. He slid to his knees, threw out an arm, brushing away as much of the small debris as possible, and lowered her to the floor. His hand held in front of her mouth detected no breath. Cobham struggled to

remember. Taking a deep breath, he leaned forward and blew it past her soft lips. At least she was still warm. He forced four more breaths into her and stopped for a moment to catch his own. What else had the doctor done? He vaguely remembered the man leaning forward and placing his hands on the chest of the victim and pressing down. After two more quick breaths for Kassandra, he stared briefly at his hands held above her trying to remember how to place them. Before he could figure it out, her eyes flicked open and Kassandra took a deep shuddering breath. Cobham froze.

"Constable, whatever you were planning on doing, it won't be necessary."

He leaned back and took a deep breath of his own.

"And you could consider getting off of me now as well."

Apologizing profusely he helped her to her feet and into the chair.

As Kassandra pinned her hair back once again, she found her way to her feet. "We need to go to the docks."

"Are you sure that you are all right? You were... well you were dead there for a while," Cobham stammered, giving her some room.

"And now I am not, thanks to you. Let's go, Mandilla told me where we need to go."

Cobham gestured her ahead of him as they turned to exit the house. "Mandilla told you? I must confess, ma'am, that I heard nothing."

"Well, Constable, the dead do not talk as such, for they no longer have any breath, but when they are embodied in the ectoplasm, their lips still move. I have made a study of lip reading and am exceptionally accurate in what I observe. She was being held at a large white building on the North side of the docks."

"That sounds as if it were the temple of the Sisters of Perceptual Emotion."

"Hmm, does make one wonder, doesn't it?" Exiting the building they started down the alleyway through the fog and shadows once more, heading toward the docks. The low growl of a dirigible hummed overhead, making the windows shake in their casements. Cobham looked up but could see nothing. "By the way, Constable, what did you find on the desk while I was communing?"

Cobham reached into his pocket and pulled out the crumpled paper. The name on the bottom of the receipt was Jamie Bersag. He handed the sheet to Kassandra. "He's a low-rate thug and one of the first ones we picked up out of his mind on this new drug. What was he doing visiting your friend?"

"Not friend, fellow practitioner. I have my suspicions that he may have helped in her abduction."

The roadway pitched downward and they descended to the docks. The fog was even thicker here and once again the same rank odor of the sea that had briefly hung in Mandilla's home stung Cobham's nostrils. Ahead, the lights from the temple appeared out of the haze. There was a low thumping sound that echoed among the buildings that sat on the rickety piers of the dock. A plume of steam rose from behind the temple to merge into the all-enshrouding mists. The very same cart that had nearly knocked them down in the street was parked to one side. Cobham led them down a side alley and around toward the back of the building.

"Are we taking another page from our prior experience, Constable?"

"Let's just say that caution may be the wisest choice in this case. What else did you learn about where Mandilla was taken?"

"We need to go down, to the lowest level of the building, almost to the water level."

Cobham felt the vibration of the unseen engine in the iron of the railing as they descended the rusting spiral staircase. At its base they found a grated walkway leading under the edge of the building and the dock. A lit rectangle of a window showed their destination. Cobham gestured Kassandra to one side. He slid open the tin door and peered into the window through the corner of his eye. The large dimly lit room beyond was filled with strange equipment. There was no one in sight. Reaching around to his belt, Cobham pulled out his revolver and made sure each of the three rotating barrels were primed. Then, with the gun ahead of him, he pulled open the door and stepped inside.

Once again the sickly sweet smell and mixture of ozone assailed his nose. After a quick sweep of the room ensured him that he was alone, Cobham walked to the single door in the far wall. He found a wooden box of small, silvered containers by the door. They were a match for the containers discovered with the Singers. Picking one out, he leaned it against the door and then turned back to motion Kassandra to come. Instead he found her already inside standing over of the machinery. Shaking his head, he strode up to her. A metal tray pierced by a single hole at its center was suspended over a round white vat. Overhead snaked cabling that ran to bubbling glass jars and a five-pointed array of brass knobs. What was he looking at? He stooped down to the vat. Inside was a drop of silvery liquid that gave off the pungent aroma he'd smelled. He dipped his finger into the liquid and raised it to his lips.

It didn't have a taste so much as a wisp of potential that crackled along his gums. Something just outside of his hearing vibrated in his head. Kassandra leaned over and shook his shoulder hard. Standing up swiftly he struck the suspended tray. The resulting sound echoed through the room. As he rubbed at his head with his free hand, Kassandra guided him away from the machine. "Be quiet," she hissed as they reached the left-hand wall.

"What does all this mean?" Cobham asked bewildered, leaning against the tin sheeting.

"It means all my fellow practitioners are likely dead. Good people died here, Constable, but what I don't understand is why would anyone want to harvest ectoplasm from us?"

Cobham shook his head at her statement. "You're saying the drug that I've been dealing with is ectoplasm? The strange silvery material you called into existence at Mandilla's?"

"Somewhat perceptive, Constable. Yes that is it exactly, but it does not answer my question, I fear."

"Why do they sing?"

Kassandra replied softly, "Ectoplasm is the insulation between our world and that of the departed. It vibrates with the music of the other side, the song of the seraphim. The seraphim are creatures who are direct expressions of the Divine will, so their music is an expression of that will. The glossolalia your singers are experiencing is the result of drinking the ectoplasm and hearing the song of the seraphim."

"Most of the folks who are singing are pretty far from divine," responded Cobham, "and this is all a damn sight too impossible for my taste."

She smiled at him briefly. "My dear Constable, we don't get to choose what we prefer is real. We have to learn how to deal with what reality gives us. You've heard a choir before, haven't you? That many voices together approximate something that no individual could accomplish."

"So you're saying that a certain number of singers comes closer to a divine sound? And therefore, because it is divine, one is compelled to listen?"

"Well done. But it still does nothing to answer the question of—"

A sound interrupted her and Cobham stepped forward in front of Kassandra. The bottle he'd placed against the door had fallen over. Even now he could see the edge of the door coming closed. They were discovered.

Cobham bolted for the doorway. He threw open the tin-sheeted door and found himself in front of another walkway. Ahead of him the small form of a Sister of Perceptual Emotion ran toward the temple. Without hesitation he threw himself after her. The walkway juddered under his feet. He caught up with the sister just before she reached the stairway leading up the side of the temple. Reaching out, he hooked an arm through hers and swung her about in the limited room of the walkway so that she ended behind him.

They stood there a moment considering each other and then the sister drew a long knife with a hooked tip from her vestments and lunged at Cobham. He took a swift step backward certain he couldn't avoid the blow, but it never fell. Instead the sister stumbled forward to her knees and Cobham could see Kassandra standing triumphantly behind her, the handle of the umbrella hooked around the sister's ankle. Scrambling to her feet, the sister lost her habit and Cobham found himself staring at her before stepping out of the way of her next rush. Plunging toward him, the sister missed her target and flipped over the side of the railing to plummet into the waves below. Kassandra stepped up to the edge and looked down. Turning to Cobham, she asked, "Why did she have a mustache?"

Cobham instantly recognized the knife and the tattoo on the sister's upper lip was the final clue. His eyes narrowed. "She was a Southron Islander. When the women join the men in a war party, they dye themselves a tattoo mustache to show they will be as brave any man. I recognized that knife immediately. The hook on the end helps to gut fish. We should have a look at exactly what is going on in this temple of theirs."

As he bounded up the steps he could hear Kassandra trying to keep up. "But aren't we at peace with the Southron Islands?" she asked.

"We may have ceded their islands back to them, but all they remember is the occupation. There are several tribes out there in the archipelago who have sworn never to forgive the Empire."

"Constable, the Sisters of Perceptual Emotion established themselves here two years ago, correct?"

"You're right, ma'am, and with their habits, gloves, and cloaks no one guessed who they were. We all believed the lie that they wore the holy vestments to keep themselves pure, hah! But still, what is their game? Gain a hold over the locals by addicting them to ectoplasm?"

"We're missing something, Constable, something important."

Then they arrived at a balcony on the side of the temple. Cobham carefully opened the door and they slid within. There was a light at the end of the hallway they entered and the sound of a multitude of voices lifted in song. The song caught at Cobham's mind with silvery hooks, pulling at him, wanting him, desiring him. His knees collapsed and he fell into the draperies covering the balcony doorway. The heavy material sheathed him enough to dampen the insidious music. He quickly fumbled in his pocket pulling out the additional rounds for his pistol wrapped in gun cotton and began tearing off bits from the larger piece. Rolling it up, he slid it into his right ear and then repeated the process with his left. Before regaining his feet, he tore off two more bits. Wadding them up, he started down the hall in search of Kassandra.

She was right up against the railing of a gallery. Below her were masses of the assembled singers. They stood there, heads lolling to one side and their mouths open; out poured an unending stream of glossolalia. At the far side of the expanse,

Cobham could see several sisters huddled around a machine waiting expectantly. He caught Kassandra's elbow and she struggled briefly. One of the sisters reached forward to the machine and drew from it a foot-long black cylinder. She held it up briefly to the light staring at its surface. Then her head tipped to one side and Cobham realized she had seen his struggles with Kassandra. He saw her mouth working and she pointed toward their place on the balcony. The remaining sisters turned as one and started from the altar toward the rear of the gathering. Their leader tucked the cylinder into her vestments and ran toward the front of the temple.

Cobham pulled Kassandra back from the brink as she struggled with him, throwing elbows and kicking. In the hallway she seemed to calm slightly and turned to him, all violence gone. The look she gave him now was one of complete and absolute submission. Suddenly, he was certain she would do anything he asked of her. He had a brief memory of her soft lips pressed against his as he'd breathed her back to life and his face flushed red. Then he took the pieces of gun cotton and pushed them into her ears. The gaze that she cast at him now was shocked, but swiftly turned to anger. With two swift steps she retrieved her umbrella from where it had fallen on the floor and stepped to his side once more. Cobham breathed a sigh of relief and led them out of the door onto the balcony on the side of the temple. There he tore the strips from his ears. Considering them a moment, he thrust them into a pocket.

The stairway continued upward and Cobham led the way. At the top they discovered a catwalk that continued to the front of the temple. Cobham's mind worked furiously. He thought he knew what the sister had in her hand and perhaps a reason for all of this. At the front of the temple he stopped—there was nowhere further to go. Kassandra caught at his shoulder, peering around him. Below them a carriage pulled away from the temple racing toward the center of Amphyra.

Next to them rose the bell tower of the temple and between its porticos could be seen the long cords of the bell rope descending to the floor below. Cobham strode forward and pulled up the bell rope. His hands drew the cord into the familiar pattern of a bowline and then reached out for Kassandra. "Come on, we've no time." He only hesitated a moment when she joined him and threw her arms around him. That first step over the edge took some courage and after the next step he vowed not to look again at Kassandra's panicked eyes.

"You are quite silent, Constable. Whatever are you thinking?"

"I'm thinking the ambassador is in danger." Only a few more feet remained until the level of the street. "I'm thinking that this was all an elaborate plan to affect the way people think—specifically one person, the ambassador, since he would have access to His Majesty himself." He was shouting now as the bells rang with every bounce of their descent. Cobham's feet hit the cobblestone and he cursed as he realized that a sizeable crowd had formed, called by the bells. Taking Kassandra's arm, he pulled her across the packed street to the opposite side and down the nearest alley.

At the steamline that rose against the brick wall, he stopped so they could catch their breath. "I'm thinking that we're the only ones who've discovered this threat, and we might need some help." He fumbled his key and then grasped the brass cylinder in the pneumatic steam tube. Using the parchment within and its attendant charcoal pencil, he swiftly scribbled a brief note to Avery. Sealing up the cylinder, Cobham shoved it into the emergency steam tube to the Constabulary. They stood there a moment in the alley looking at the crowd in front of the temple. There was no escape that way. In the same instant they both happened to look up. As smile grew on Kassandra's face when Cobham said, "I'm thinking we need to go the last place they'll look for us—the rooftops."

✠

Stumbling now that his bravado gave way to exhaustion, Cobham led them across the back roof of the opera house. Their merry run across the rooftops had brought them here as quickly as possible. Below, the ambassador would be enjoying the performance of the Amazing Audible Cylindrograph, but Cobham doubted the sounds were anything other than glossolalia. Pulling out his weapon, he checked its readiness. Looking back at Kassandra, who had gamely kept up with his mad run, he motioned for her to plug her ears once more. Then he pulled out the gun cotton and saw to his own. With everything gone silent, he spared a look down to see the Constabulary wagons racing around the corner. Taking a deep breath, he leapt the remaining distance to the exterior balcony of the opera house.

As he heard Kassandra join him, Cobham kicked at the join of the doors and they sprung open. Inside the plush hallway he hesitated briefly. There were two constables in a doorway ahead of him, but neither reacted to his entrance. Were they already too late? He plunged forward between them and out into the ambassador's box. The man himself turned in his plush velvet chair at Cobham's entrance, startled. Below on the stage was a very familiar device, the light reflecting from the shiny black cylinder that revolved amongst complicated brass elements. Stepping up to the rail, Cobham raised his pistol and took aim, resting his arms on the polished wood. He felt rather than heard a thump as the gun went off. The cylinder and its attendant machine shattered into spinning fragments that scattered over the stage. Stepping back, Cobham nearly fell over the form of the ambassador. Kassandra barely restrained him against the floor.

Something caught Cobham's eye. There was a dark piece of cloth in the ear of the ambassador. Cobham hesitated and in that second, the ambassador threw Kassandra to one side and staggered to his feet. As Cobham struggled to spin the barrel on his revolver, the black-haired man sprang between the guards into the corridor. Cobham pulled out one of the earplugs in frustration. Kassandra grasped at his sleeve. "He must have betrayed His Majesty to the Southron Islanders. He's getting away!"

"Not if I can help it, he's not," growled Cobham as he leapt over the chair after the ambassador. A flicker of a curtain caught his eye. The doors to the balcony were open wider than before. In a moment he'd cleared the remaining distance to the balcony and plunged out into the foggy night once more. But now the night was lit with red by the flare in the ambassador's hand. All of the windows of the opera house shook in sympathy as a dirigible rapidly dropped out of the sky. An anchor line snaked down and the grappling hook on its end snared the railing.

In three steps Cobham threw the high official to the floor. As the fans of the massive ship scattered dust and debris, he thrust the barrel of his pistol against the ambassador's temple. The red eye and clenched fists of the Southron Islands symbol shone on the metal sides of the airship in the light of the dropped flare. Why had he never noticed the similarity to the emblem of the Sisters of Perceptual Emotion? Cobham wondered. For several moments that tableaux held with no one moving. Cobham hoped the men aboard the dirigible realized that their gambit had failed. Suddenly, with a great deal of shouting, Avery and a crowd of constables pushed past Kassandra to fill the balcony. A flash of light from the knife in Kassandra's hand caught his attention as she cut through the anchor line. Just as swiftly as it arrived, the dirigible lifted upward in a blast of air.

"Avery," Cobham called out, "arrest this man."

Reaching for the prisoner's wrists, Avery flinched. "But he's the ambassador."

"No," Cobham replied, coming to a stop by Kassandra. "He *was* the ambassador. Now he's just a traitor."

"You can prove nothing, you bastard," shouted their prisoner.

"Fortunately, I have a witness," Cobham stated, looking at Kassandra. "Take him away, Avery, and put him in a cell next to some singers. We'll talk to him in the morning. I have a funny feeling he'll tell us everything we need to know." He turned and leaned against the balcony, taking a welcome breath, and stared at the city below, its lights shimmering in the fog. "So, are we done?" Cobham asked Kassandra.

"Well, Constable, remember what I said. Sometimes strange clusters like grapes. If we're fortunate we've reached the last of the bunch."

"Well enough," he replied and together they enjoyed the moment of silence that spread as the other constables departed.

AMBERGRIS ON ICE

THE INCESSANT COLD WAS ALMOST WORSE THAN THEIR DESCENT TO THE wreckage of the dirigible. Whipping gusts in the early light of dawn spun Constable Cobham Peckwith and the others about as they dangled over the ocean in the cargo drop. They struck the surface of the iceberg a solid blow, tumbling the *Sharpshin's* first mate Airman Sparrowknife and Madame Leyden against the lines. Cobham reached out a hand to the lady and Kassandra grasped at his thick gloves. Her clear blue eyes peered out from under the hood of her parka. She seemed out of place here in jodhpurs and thick mukluk boots, having eschewed her perennial dress. But there was something in her gaze, a brightness that assured Cobham she was enjoying the adventure. He wished he could say the same for himself. As a constable, Cobham had every expectation of pounding the streets of his homeport city of Amphyra, keeping order and maintaining the safety of the inhabitants of His Majesty's lands in the New World. But ever since he'd met the medium, with her unusual talent for communing with the dead, his life had become anything but typical.

The wind brought tiny shards of ice flying along the surface of the berg into his unguarded face. But that wasn't the worst of it; Bornesun, the captain of their airship, had neglected to mention the way the iceberg would move. When Cobham peered out into the morning, he could watch the horizon tip back and forth. What looked like an island was a cork afloat on a frigid sea. *We don't belong here*, he thought. Kassandra moved a few steps forward to stand beside him and another thought crossed his mind, *Do I really want to keep doing this*? Working with her challenged what he accepted as real, every day. Sure he had already seen plenty of the odd and strange out on the streets. In most cases though he'd found a sad, tawdry explanation more often than not linked to human stupidity or depravity. But there were always those circumstances that made no sense. Cobham waited for the airman to approach them, looking at Kassandra as she stared at the shifting horizon. As a medium who spoke to the departed, dearly or otherwise, she knew a great deal about those oddities, in fact she made it her business.

When Sparrowknife passed them, Cobham followed Kassandra toward the remains of the dirigible. A discovery such as this must have given the commanders of His Majesty's Aerofleet the fits, he mused. After all, only New Britain, the South Islanders, and the Mexateca were capable of building such a vehicle. Cobham couldn't quite fathom the arcane series of connections that the Directorate of Security followed to ascertain that he and Madam Leyden were the best suited to delve into this mystery, but it wasn't his place to question. Perhaps if he had they would not now be drifting toward the artic.

A tug on the line at his waist brought him from his brief reverie. Wil Sparrowknife strode ahead of them and was the anchor to the rope tied about their middles. Curving metal spars arched over their heads. The vehicle's remnants were deceptive when seen from above. With its bulk strewn along the rugged, bluish-white surface of the iceberg, the dirigible stretched out longer than two of Amphyra's city blocks. Sparrowknife had stopped to stare as well. With the wind the only sound, it came to Cobham just how removed from the world they were. The airman gestured them closer and they huddled together to talk.

"There's something quite wrong here," Sparrowknife started and then hesitated.

"Yes, I'd expected a great deal more wreckage," Cobham said.

"No, what I mean is there something missing." The airman turned once again to look at the wreckage.

"The bodies are gone."

Cobham turned sharply to Kassandra. What she said was true. *Where was the crew of at least forty needed to man such a dirigible?* Cobham pondered.

"With all of this wind the remains might have been scoured off of the berg into the ocean," Sparrowknife answered. "What I mean is, there's no cladding on the structure. Even if the dirigible exploded, there should still be some of the exterior sheeting someplace attached to the framework. But no matter where I look, I can't see a shred."

Cobham turned on his heel. The first mate was correct and so was Kassandra. "What's so important about the cladding?"

"Well it would have had a huge blazon of the aircraft's owner, at least. Also each nation makes theirs a bit different, even the paint used could tell me whose this is," Sparrowknife responded, crouching down to scuff at the snow in the hopes of finding anything more.

It almost felt to Cobham as if the clues to the cause had vanished. "Well, guess we won't be asking any of the dead fellows anything then, Kassandra, will we?" he commented.

"Look over here," Sparrowknife interrupted. He'd stepped under the arching support structure of the dirigible.

On the far side, in amongst the spans of the frame, was a large, gaping hole. As Cobham stared in the direction the airman indicated a pattern began to emerge. The supports were all bent and twisted away from the gap. Something had struck the dirigible a killing blow.

Tapping glove tips to his lip, Sparrowknife pondered. "It's almost as if something exploded on contact with the surface of the craft."

"Do you have a weapon like that, airman?" Kassandra asked.

"Not that I know of. The *Sharpshin* is armed with two repeating cylinder guns. Larger military-class dirigibles will have mounted cannon, which can be used to fire grapeshot or chain loads. But we have nothing that explodes on impact."

"What could bring down an aircraft of this size?" Kassandra continued.

Sparrowknife hesitated a moment, thinking. "Fire, a lightning strike, a tornado, and our mysterious explosion, too." The airman's words trailed off. He stopped and turned about in a circle.

Cobham felt the man's unease as well, an animal instinct reacting to unknown danger. When he glanced at Kassandra, she'd crossed her arms, shoving her gloves under them. In her eyes he saw that she felt the same.

"I don't know how much more we're going to find here," she offered in a grim tone.

At a loud crack of gunfire, they all turned back toward the airship. High above them the captain was waving his arms over his head. Sparrowknife didn't hesitate. "All right, let's get back to the ship. The captain wouldn't signal us unless it was urgent."

As the cargo lift swung back and forth, Cobham saw at the edge of his visibility a gray haze hanging over the waterline. After a moment he realized what he was seeing. They were approaching the northern shore of Aurora. The massive island lay close to the Arctic Circle, in the gap between the Old World and the New. Cobham shivered at the thought of the Old World. The abandoned seat of Edward's empire lay there in ruins along with an entire series of lands long overgrown and filled with the bones of the victims of the ancient Death. A few brave traders pillaged the forgotten lands for treasure and paid the price by contracting the plague. This was the closest he'd ever been. Cobham hoped to never approach any nearer. Now he could even see the enormous pieces of ice as they calved away from a glacier on the shoreline and cascaded into the freezing water below. The iceberg carrying the remains of the dirigible was several leagues away from the shore. Their evidence was about to be lost, perhaps for forever.

"What's that, Airman?" Kassandra asked, pointed farther along the shoreline at single flicker of reflection.

"I have no idea," Sparrowknife responded staring at the spark along the shoreline at the edge of their vision. The cargo lift swung back and forth, causing them all to reach for the netting. "Seems like the captain's noticed it as well. We'll know soon enough."

✠

The closer they approached to the shore, the more trouble Cobham had discerning what lay below them. After turning the airship away from the iceberg, the captain was unable to reacquire the location of the mysterious flashes of light. Captain Bornesun brought the airship down the coastline, beyond the glacier to a large circular bay. All along the rubble-lined beach were immense white cylinders with tapered ends. Cobham counted more than twenty before stopping. Whatever the objects were, they lay on the shoreline with their anteriors in the splashing surf.

"They're leviathans," Sparrowknife said in a quiet tone.

Cobham found that if he stared long enough he could see the fins on the sides of the carcasses. Here and there conjoined flippers of the beast's tails bobbed in the surf.

"I've heard of them beaching themselves but I've never seen anything like this," Bornesun added. "Look at that beast. It's more than twice the size of our downed dirigible." Bornesun's words trailed off as he brought the spyglass to his eye once more. Wrinkles spread across his forehead. "Well that explains the flash. There's a settlement inland from the beach. All the buildings are covered in ice rime. Makes them hard to pick out, but for the glint of the sun. They appear to have some sort of balloon on a tether."

He handed the spyglass to Kassandra, who stood next to him. Cobham watched her stare intently for a moment or two. Then she inhaled; her breath catching.

"If I'm correct, the man walking down the beach toward the leviathans is Sir Sante Moore. He's well known as an oceanographic biologist, historical chemist, and a Renaissance man of the sciences. He's also waving us in. Looks as if we've been seen."

When she handed the glass back to the captain, Kassandra walked behind him to come up next to Cobham. Leaning close she whispered, "He's also a pompous ass." Then she hesitated and added, "And a friend of my father's," as her eyes drifted away from his gaze.

The twitchy sensation in his nerves wouldn't abate, so Cobham took a moment to retrieve his three-barrel revolver from his travel case, tucking it into one of the deep pockets of his parka. He felt a slight bit guilty doing it out of Kassandra's view, but it calmed his nerves. At the edge of the cargo area Cobham confronted Kassandra. "This is no place for a lady."

"Be that as it may, I am here and I will go where I please. Besides Moore's familiarity with my father may serve our purpose."

"Kassandra, be reasonable."

"Constable, my father does all of his adventuring from an armchair with a glass of sherry in a half-drunken stupor. He was one of the brightest lights in the scientific pantheon. When he stopped 'doing' he became trapped in his brick manse. All of his brilliance spilled out into lax dreaming. I'll do my work on my feet, if you please."

Cobham stared at her back as Kassandra moved away to converse with the captain. In that mere moment he'd learned more about what drove her than in all of their acquaintance.

Once again they descended in the cargo lift.

"I'm surprised the captain isn't joining us," Kassandra said, watching the ground approach.

"Don't be," was Sparrowknife's answer. He looked up at the airship above them, shading gray eyes with a hand. "He doesn't leave the ship."

Cobham turned to the first mate. "Ever?"

"Not unless ordered to. The *Sharpshin* is a ship in His Majesty's Aerofleet. As captain, he can do as he likes." Sparrowknife hesitated. "Bornesun says the ground doesn't feel right anymore."

Not finding an adequate response, Cobham considered their destination. There were a number of long buildings with rounded roofs. He could count more than a dozen men walking about the complex. A well-worn path led down to the beach below and its unusual contents. He watched four men, each carrying a crate toward the farthest building, moving along at a steady pace. Suddenly, the lead man pitched forward, missing his footing.

This fellow's crate flew from his hands and landed in the snow next to the path. The reactions of the men were what caught Cobham's attention. Each turned away from the impact, crouching over their own crate. They all froze in place. As the ground grew closer, Cobham watched the three men with the crates edge their way around their fallen comrade, hurrying toward the out building. Only when they were gone did the remaining bearer regain his burden and follow. Turning to his companions, Cobham realized he was the sole witness of the incident. Grasping his chin, Cobham wondered, *just what was that about?*

The cargo lift continued its descent. Learning from last time, Cobham took the impact of landing by flexing his knees. He offered Kassandra an arm as Sparrowknife led them off of the cargo lift. As Sir Sante Moore hustled up to them, the lift began its return to the airship. Cobham looked up at it a moment. Even though they were on solid ground, he still had the feeling that things were moving out of his control.

"Welcome to my little corner of the world," bellowed Moore, smiling expansively. He was a big man and the fur of the bear skin parka he wore rustled in the wind, which tore sparks from the edge of the pipe in his outstretched hand. He flipped the silver damper down, settling it once more between large, yellowed teeth as he leaned forward to greet each one of them. Sparrowknife and Cobham each received a wringing handshake and Kassandra a bow over her proffered hand.

As Kassandra made their introductions, Cobham took the moment to review Moore's companions. There were several British fellows present in the front ranks, one even carrying the perennial tri-lion banner. *Of course*, thought Cobham, glancing at the sight of the *Sharpshin* hanging overhead. With its blazons as one of His Majesty's Airships, there was little doubt as to from whence Moore's visitors hailed. He wasn't surprised that Moore flew the colors as well. But behind these good fellows were several others whose darker complexions and beetling black brows belied a different lineage.

Sparrowknife caught his glance. Stepping closer, he whispered, "Antelaunders, they live close to the arctic to the west of New Britain and hunt the seal and white bears. As to why they're here, besides their familiarity with this cold, that's a fine question. Besides they are known to have several unsavory habits."

Cobham caught Moore's eyes turning toward them. He clapped a hand to Sparrowknife's back and led the airman forward. He gave the airman a sharp look and pasted a false smile on his face. "You'll have to forgive us, Sir Moore; we're still not quite as used to the rigors of this land as you are. Is there somewhere out of the weather where we might converse?"

"Weather? My dear sir, this is a fine and pleasant day. You should see it when Mother Nature becomes unruly. In reality, you can't. Everything becomes as white and as thick as cream." Moore laughed, a hand over his heart. "First I would like to show you our fabulous discovery, the leviathan graveyard."

Their host turned back to Kassandra. "So your father was Casimir Leyden? He would have loved this expedition, and he would have been astounded by what we've found. Please come with me, my dear. As his daughter you will have special insight into the wonders we've discovered."

Kassandra's eyes sparkled with interest as she took Moore's proffered arm. Wheeling about, the large man led the party down the pathway toward the beach. As a constable, Cobham was comfortable asking questions of others and himself until he had a clear view of the circumstances. He wasn't about to stop now. "It's a bit odd given our destination that we weren't told of your expedition before we left, Sir Moore."

"I do believe you are mistaking the nature of our venture, good sir," Moore tossed over his shoulder as they walked on. "We are a private expedition, not one of His Majesty's. Funded by a concerned group of dedicated individuals, we are able to practice pure scientific investigation. We can explore without proving that there are practical applications to our discoveries or being hedged by puritanical views."

Cobham turned back for a moment, looking at the rest of the group. Now that they were on the decline toward the beach, he could see more of the rest of their contingent. His suspicions were confirmed. The men in the rear had small blunderbusses strapped to their backs, their brass bells glinting in the harsh arctic light. *Are they for the white bears or the visitors?* he mused.

As they approached the leviathans, the reality of the beasts' size was brought home. In cross section, the creatures were as tall as the first story of a building. Their bulk stretched away in either direction. There was a faint, unusual musk in the air. Cobham's lips pursed. He'd been expecting something more pungent perhaps. Then the obvious struck him. The leviathans must have frozen the whole way through. That was when Moore led them up to the side of the nearest cetacean. Grasping at a cord, he drew up the oilskin door flap, which concealed a tunnel running into the purplish marbled interior of the beast. Kassandra stood there a moment; her eyes wide like a child's, full of wonder. She stepped forward into the golden light of a hanging lantern. Cobham spared a glance backward, then followed Moore and Sparrowknife into the belly of the beast.

Surrounded by layers of blubber and muscle, Cobham did have to admit that the shelter from the perpetual wind was better than before. However, the small lanterns did nothing for the chill. Rather their flickering light cast a haze of smoke and pungent musk. Cobham looked down, discovering the walkway was covered in a layer of gravel, tinted crimson by leviathan blood. His introspection cost him a moment and it allowed the others to continue further along the tunnel. Taking advantage of the opportunity and giving in to his curious nature, he looked about further.

A few steps forward found another tunnel opening on the right that led toward the leviathan's head. Stepping inside, Cobham walked along until he found another canvas flap door covering the entrance to a wide room carved into the beast's flesh. There was something different about the floor here. While still bearing some of the gravel, it was smooth with a metallic sheen that flickered in the light. Cobham stepped closer to the wall and pried at the edge of the odd material. It bent and flexed in his hand. Finding a corner, he worked it back and forth until a piece broke off.

The dim lighting gave him a poor view of the mysterious substance, so he placed it into his side pocket for further investigation. Standing up, Cobham noticed stacks of material projecting from the sides of the room. These were so coated in ice; he couldn't discern their interiors. He brushed off some of the rime, finding a projection. Cobham struck the piece a quick blow and it fell to the ground. Stooping down to pick up his discovery, he heard approaching footsteps. Pulling his handkerchief from his pocket, he quickly wrapped up the second piece of evidence, stowing it in his breast pocket. Two of the Antelaunders stood in the doorway. This time the blunderbusses were no longer shouldered, but pointed in his direction.

Cobham raised his hands, pasting a smile on his face. Their dark eyes searched both him and the room until Sante Moore shouldered his way between them, putting a hand on each of the brass bells of the guns to tip their aim toward the floor.

"Constable, we lost you. I understand that it may be in your nature to investigate, but perhaps you should stay with us. My associates here have some odd beliefs. Since they've been subsisting on leviathan meat since our arrival, they can be somewhat protective of their victuals." Moore gestured Cobham forward, taking his arm to lead him between the Antelaunders. Cobham hadn't missed the furtive glance the man made about the room to see if its contents were disturbed.

Cobham was led off to rejoin the others. He noticed that none of the British had joined their party. Rather there were two more Antelaunders, in addition to those following Moore and himself. A glance over his shoulder found their guards once more shouldering their blunderbusses. Moore led them into what Cobham imagined was the leviathan's stomach. Kassandra and Sparrowknife stood clustered around a piece of canvas tacked to a wall. The top half was a series of inked-in lines that must represent the tunnels carved through the beast. The sketches on the lower half were of the leviathan's internal organs. Kassandra drew her fingers back and forth across the image, her lips pursed in thought. For a moment Cobham could imagine a younger version of her, fascinated by one of her father's experiments.

Moore shattered Cobham's reverie by clapping his gloved hands together. "So what do you think of my discovery so far?"

Before Cobham could reply, Kassandra stepped into the conversational void. "What you've accomplished here is truly amazing, Sir Moore. You've laid out more about the physiology of these nearly mythical beasts than anyone before. Your methods are very inventive, crossing mining with dissection to deal with such a large subject." Cobham saw her hesitate a moment, then turn and continue with a tilt of her head, "What surprises me is with all of the leviathan blubber here, you've chosen something else to fuel your lamps."

Moore's head jerked slightly. He broke into a laugh. "I should have known that Casmir's daughter would notice the subtleties. It is true we could burn leviathan oil, but why go through the trouble of rendering that when we discovered a tar pit a short distance inland? With less work we are able to treat the oil there so that it burns for our purposes. Now I think I've subjected you to enough of the chill, let us retire to somewhere warmer." The large man spun on his heel, leading them out of the frozen tunnels into the wan sunlight.

They exited on the opposite side of the leviathan. Cobham spotted another flap door on the next remains in line. Moore's party must be exploring several of the beast's innards. Sparrowknife stopped and looked about in the open, his nose wrinkling. "Storm's coming," he stated, settling his parka's hood about his head.

"That's very perceptive of you, Airman. We'll probably have to reel in the weather balloon soon so it doesn't get damaged." Turning to the others he continued, "The storms here are abrupt and always dangerous. It would be best for us to retire to the main camp as soon as possible."

The skyline behind them had grown hazy and vague. Cobham thought back to stories of cold so bad that spittle froze before hitting the ground. Now he really wanted to be inside. As they turned back toward the buildings, Cobham noticed a repetitive thumping sound that he'd missed before. Perhaps between the leviathans, with the wind damped down, it was more audible. As they trudged up from the beach, the noise grew closer.

Suddenly, a group of four men came scrambling down the path; two of them carried their blunderbusses in hand. Cobham felt little doubt as to the direction of their aim. The others carried between them the remains of the aforementioned weather balloon. Cobham cast a quick glance about; the *Sharpshin* was nowhere to be seen. Sparrowknife gave him a pointed look, having just come to the same conclusion.

"I'm worried, Mr. Cobham. The captain wouldn't just leave us behind. He'd have a solid reason to go. We just don't know what it is." Sparrowknife said quietly.

As the men drew nearer, Cobham noticed a long line of holes in the balloon. Something that one of the repeaters mentioned by Sparrowknife would be capable accomplishing. He also noted that along with an aerometer and barometer, the balloon's payload included a heliograph. *Just who was the expedition signaling?* he wondered.

Sante Moore let out a long sigh. Turning back to his guests, annoyance rearranged his features. "I had hoped it would not come to this. But it can't be helped. Your airship captain has taken things into his own hands. He was a bit more resourceful than I expected and escaped, leaving you behind. Gentlemen, hand over your weapons please. Come, let's not make this anymore disagreeable than it need be. I'm afraid my associates are not fluent in British. They may simply fire first as their only regard is for my safety."

Cobham assessed their situation as he reached for his revolver. There were just too many. While he suspected that Sparrowknife would be a good man to have in a scuffle, he wanted Kassandra involved in none of this. He handed over his bone-handled knife as well. Sparrowknife proffered up a small pistol and several knives. The armed Antelaunders marched behind the party now as Sante Moore led the group in the direction of the odd thumping noise.

After passing through the buildings, they turned a corner to discover the originator of the sound. Inside a hollow carved out from the surrounding snow lay a large iron machine. Spangles of orange rust tinged the dull brown color of it. Chuffing steam, one giant lever arm thrust out over and over sideways. The resultant clang of its extension echoed throughout the encampment. *This must be some sort of pump*, Cobham thought. Beyond the device, the ground sloped downward into the tar pit that Moore had mentioned.

"So, is that where we're going to end up? Sunk in the tar?" Sparrowknife snarled, taking a step toward Moore. The bell of a blunderbuss swung around to thump against the airman's chest. He never took his eyes from Moore's. Cobham's appreciation of the young man went up a notch.

But Sparrowknife wasn't done. "Miss Kassandra, don't be fooled by him. There's plenty of dirty work afoot here. If he hasn't done it himself, then he's seen fit to approve of it. Those leviathans didn't die by themselves."

"Oh, I am certain that I question our host's qualities, but whatever do you mean by that, Airman?"

While answering her, Sparrowknife still glared at Moore. "I may not have ever seen a beaching before, but it would be a true oddity if all of the poor creatures were to drag themselves into a nice regular row where their heads were in a line despite how large they were. Besides that, why would they all end up on their backs? I suspect that it's because if we saw their tops we'd find a hole very similar to that on the wrecked dirigible. Isn't that right, Sir Moore?"

Cobham watched Sante Moore unclasp the pipe from his lips to tap its contents out into the snow. The big man put it away, each one of his moments stiff with restraint as the scientist struggled to hold his tongue. "Well, young man, before we had an instance where I could have told you that the *Sharpshin* disappeared mysteriously. Now that's no longer the case."

"So what's he doing digging in all of the leviathans?" Cobham asked.

Moore was silent, his face now twisted into a scowl.

"Ambergris," Kassandra answered. "Leviathans are known to produce ambergris in a regular fashion whereas in their whale relatives it is somewhat rare. Ambergris is worth quite a bit of money—money that could be used to continue to fund such a project." She watched their captor intently. "But that's not it, is it, Sante? You've found another use for the ambergris haven't you?"

"It is a very unique substance, given its volatility." Moore said with a smile. "In fact, mixing it with certain elements taken from ancient Greek alchemical texts makes it an excellent catalyst."

"Let me have a guess, a catalyst that could be used as weapon?" interjected Kassandra. "Such as...Greek fire?"

Moore continued without acknowledging her interruption. "The catalyst mixed with the refined oil from the tar pit makes quite an explosive. Apply sufficient force to start a reaction and the mixture becomes quite destructive. That, my dear, is the weapon."

Another sound intruded on Cobham's hearing, just below the omnipresent pump. This was a drone of sorts. Sparrowknife noticed it as well. The airman's eyes flickered away from Moore to look upward. Out of the clouds came an immense dirigible, its prow low over the encampment. The long, gray cylinder of its bulk stretched into the distance.

"The *Windram* is quite an aeronaught isn't she?" Moore asked, his voice filled with pride.

"There's no such thing as an aeronaught," Sparrowknife spat.

Looking at the massive machine drifting by overhead, Cobham felt that he might just have to disagree. It was armored along the sides and bottom. Two sets of spars jutted outward at a swept-back angle bearing immense rotary fan blades that spun in a blur. Round barnacle-like protrusions harbored the barrels of cannons. The massive tail fins cut through the low-hanging clouds. He couldn't blame Bornesun for lighting out with the *Sharpshin*. The airship wouldn't stand a chance against this behemoth.

Kassandra, as always, went straight to the point, "Why, Sante? Why do all of this?"

Moore responded after a moment's thought. "The King's empire in the New World is dying. Dying because he refuses to let us grow and learn."

"That is treason," Sparrowknife said in a clipped tone.

"Spoken just like a true King's man. But in consideration of your loyalty, do you know the history that your monarch's dynasty is based upon?

"When Edward the Third and the Black Prince led the court out of the Old World to establish New Britain in the New World it was a time of great opportunity. We left behind the old ideas with the plague-ridden continent. We conquered a whole new land. We opened our arms to the survivors that made it to our shores, because we'd realized it didn't matter where one grew up. We were human and alive, that was enough. Our nation grew from the strengths of its many cultures. We experienced a renaissance, much like the old Greeks. Our scientists, artists, and philosophers all came together to create something greater than the sum of the whole."

"That's true," interjected Kassandra. "It was an age of adventure and growth."

Moore's countenance darkened as he swung toward her. "Then we conquered the entirety of the southern continent using what we'd discovered of the plague as a weapon. We pushed all of the native peoples out of our new land into the Southron Islands off of our coast. We gave them indentured servitude that might as well have been slavery."

Shaking his head, Moore pointed a finger at their party. "But we'd reached too far. Our grasp couldn't contain all of the lands we'd conquered. Now we had to try to hold onto what we'd conquered. We couldn't even do that. We gave the southern continent to the Mexateca and the Southron Islands back to their inhabitants. We also left them all of our machinery and knowledge as well. Is it any wonder they harbor resentment against us? Our proud Monarchy bred generation after generation of Edwards until achieving the present incarnation who can barely hold onto what we have. New Britain is waning. Our once great country has no future."

Moore's sudden silence after such a long diatribe caught Cobham by surprise, but he could see the tension still working in the man as he strode back and forth. This time when Moore turned back to the group of captives, his attention was focused on Cobham and Sparrowknife and as he spoke each word grew louder in volume until he shouted.

"Because I am a man of science I cannot be restrained by hidebound ideals and a lack of vision. Your tottering empire, ruled by aged, senile fools trapped in the dark bunkers of their fear trembles on its very last legs. The future will leave His Majesty behind. I don't intend to be left with him."

Shaking with anger, Moore addressed the Antelaunders, "Take them to the outbuilding by the pump and secure them there. We'll decide what needs to be done after the *Windram* comes to tether."

"My father used to speak of you as a true visionary, Sante. I wonder how he couldn't see past that to the madness," Kassandra stated as one of their guards grasped her shoulder to spin her about.

Moore turned his back on their party, starting to walk off. "Your father used to be part of my coterie," their captor called to her over his shoulder. "He used to be a believer, one of many. Disabuse yourself of the notion that I am doing this on my own, dear Kassandra. But your father, he never had the stamina to keep up with us. He was weak," Moore finished as he marched off.

✠

The dilapidated shed was a poor windbreak. Cobham could feel the incessant gusts and hear them whistling through the cracks in the building. The three prisoners huddled about the small coal brazier in the shack's center.

"This morning I walked through the wreckage of a dirigible. Now I'm in the clutches of a mad man. I really can't tell you how much I enjoy being along for the adventure, Kassandra. In the future can we possibly consider something a little bit less life-threatening?" Cobham said shoving his hands deep into the pockets of his parka, leaning closer to the brazier.

"But isn't it exciting?" she responded with a sly smile.

Before he could frame a suitable response, Cobham rammed his fingers into items that he'd discovered inside the leviathan. He pulled the metal from his pocket, holding it up before the feeble light from the fire.

"Can I see that, constable?" Sparrowknife asked. The airman turned the fragment over in his hands. "Well, there is the cladding we were looking for earlier. Where did you find it?"

"Moore is using it to line some of the rooms inside the leviathans."

"That is odd, but it does prove that Moore went back and removed the cladding and everything else from the iceberg," Sparrowknife mused. He took the metal and tossed it into the brazier. Immediately, the small fire blazed up in a puff of flame. "Must be the paint. Southrons and Mexateca sometimes use inferior paints on the exterior of their dirigibles."

"What I don't understand is the whole reason for their involvement with the wreckage," Kassandra said.

"I think we can call it an experiment," Cobham offered. "If I was to guess I would say that Sante made the discovery of the ambergris bomb some time ago. Once he was able to perfect it, he and his allies used it to kill all of the leviathans we've seen on the beach to acquire more ambergris. From there they needed to prove that it could be used as a weapon against aircraft."

"So the wreckage was from a test," Sparrowknife interjected.

"Yes, they tethered the dirigible to the iceberg. Then they dropped the bomb on it. That might be why there was nothing but the framework, they wouldn't have wasted anything else. I suppose because he is familiar with this area that Sante knew the iceberg would drift back toward Aurora. The *Windram* could be here to salvage the framework," Cobham continued.

"So now they have something with which to destroy dirigibles and airships, how perfectly awful," Kassandra said shaking her head.

Reaching for the other item, Cobham found that the ice covering the piece had melted soaking his handkerchief. Cobham thrust his hand closer to the fire and stared at what lay in his palm.

Kassandra's brow wrinkled as she poked at his hand. "Constable, wherever did you find a severed finger, inside the leviathan?"

Cobham remained silent a moment considering the stacks that the finger had come from. "There were bodies so frozen together I couldn't tell what they were. I broke off a piece before Sante and his men found me. I wonder how many there are in there..."

"Well that explains something," Sparrowknife offered. "I know how he convinced the Antelaunders to work for him. Some of them developed a taste for human flesh. Moore must be paying the cannibals that way."

"So he's got a larder full of corpses stored inside a dead leviathan. This just gets better with every passing moment. Who are they, I wonder?" Cobham asked.

"From the looks of things, I would say anyone who doesn't agree with that madman," Kassandra offered. She reached out to Cobham for the finger. He happily surrendered it to her. "Your question, constable, has another meaning. Who are the people supporting Moore? I think I may have a way to find out."

Kassandra pulled back her hood. Shrugging out of her gloves, she reached up to free the long ringlets of her red hair. Her tresses were bound up on her head in a bun transfixed by two amber-colored rods. She pulled the rods out, sparing a moment to twist her hair out of the way. Setting the rods aside near the severed digit, she reached for one of her gloves. Working the liner out, she was able to get at the woolen interior. Regaining the rods, she lay them in the liner. Then she began rub the shafts back and forth. After a few moments, Cobham could see the fibers of the wool starting to stand up as well as the loose hairs on top of Kassandra's head.

"Constable, make me some room on the floor please. I'll need a smooth area in the dirt close enough to the brazier that we'll be able to see." Cobham took off his gloves and set about scraping the detritus on the floor away from the desired area. She nodded at him when he was done, then said, "Please place the finger at the bottom closest to me." As soon as he'd dropped the severed finger on the ground, she leaned forward touching it on either end with one of the rods. A fat blue spark jumped from each rod and the finger shimmered with a slick coating of something that looked like mercury. Cobham had seen Kassandra call spirits before and knew that what he was seeing was ectoplasm, but what she intended next, he had no idea.

She held out the rods to the two men. "Airman, please write in the dirt on the left here the numbers from one to ten then the words 'yes' and 'no'. Constable, I need you to write out the letters of the alphabet here on your side." Then she leaned forward to pick up the finger. Holding it in her hands, she squeezed her eyes closed, took a breath and held it. When she breathed out, silvery ectoplasm coated her lips. It wafted out in gossamer strands in the air as if she were spewing out spider's silk. Drifting downward, the mercurial matter collected on the finger.

Both men sat back, having finished writing. Cobham found himself staring as Kassandra lay the silvery digit on the floor. He spared a glance at Sparrowknife. The airman seemed to be taking the oddity of the situation fairly well. Sparrowknife caught the look and commented, "Not to worry, constable, my auntie was well known for making simples and small tellings."

"Well, you're handling it better than I did the first time. Kassandra made everything in the room float including me and brought everything back to earth with a crash," Cobham said.

"I was using someone else's equipment, of inferior quality at that. As you see, gentlemen, quite a good deal can be accomplished with a small amount. But to business, let us see if we can establish a rapport."

The finger slid across the ground as if the surface were ice, coming to rest on Sparrowknife's scrawl for 'yes'.

"Kassandra who are we talking to?" Cobham asked.

She turned to him for a moment ignoring the finger that was speeding across the floor once again. "Constable, this is a ghost. Unlike a spirit whom I would commune with across the divide that separates the living world from those that passed on, ghosts are still anchored here by a need to achieve closure. I would guess that an untimely death at the hands of a man like Moore might qualify."

"It spelled out Cyrus," Sparrowknife interjected.

Kassandra gave Cobham a brief smile returning to the matter at hand, "So, Cyrus, can you tell us who Moore's allies are?"

Once the finger completed its macabre skating again, Cobham felt the chill in the small building increase. *Southrons still maintain a simmering hatred for their former masters*, he thought. Moore had chosen dangerous allies. Ones who were eager for such weapons and the opportunities they offered. Now they had another reason to escape. His Majesty must be warned of this new threat. Cobham turned over thoughts and plans in his mind. Time for another question, "Where are the bombs stored?" One of the primed bombs placed under the reciprocating arm of the oil pump could set the whole pit on fire destroying the pump. A bomb could even disable the massive *Windram* as well. The finger skidded away from the letters and numbers and proceeded to scratch a map into the floor indicating a long building not far from where they were held. But first they needed to escape.

"So how do we get out?" Cobham asked the obvious. The finger slid across the floor to the word "no". "Sorry, Cyrus, I suspect that's up to us. But thank you for your help so far." *Now I'm talking to a disembodied digit*, Cobham thought, stopping himself before he could wonder if the day could get any stranger.

Kassandra grinned at him for a moment, then slid a hand into her left mukluk and pulled out a long thin knife.

Sparrowknife chuckled when she handed it to him. "Lady, I do like your surprises." Standing, he made his way to the door. Taking advantage of the gaps in the walls, the airman circled the interior of the shed staring out where he could. Then he returned to the brazier. "There's only one guard. He has his back to the door. There is a simple latch I can flip open with the knife. But we'll need a distraction. Cyrus, can we prevail upon you?"

A moment later, Sparrowknife was crouched by the door, knife level with the latch. Cobham stood beside him ready to pull the door open and deal with their guard. The disembodied finger of their ghostly ally slid under the gap of the door. Cobham spared a moment to imagine what it might be like to see the silvery digit sliding between one's legs like a hyperactive slug. Then he heard a spate of unintelligible words. Sparrowknife flipped the knife and the door slid open far enough for Cobham to force his fingers into the gap. Pulling backward, Cobham felt the door give as the guard lost his feet.

The Antelaunder fell back over Sparrowknife's crouched form, his head struck the brazier, sending coals flying. Sparrowknife leapt to his feet, scrambling for the man's blunderbuss. His instincts coming into play, Cobham pulled the guard to his feet, swung back, and roundhoused the Antelaunder hard enough that the man bounced off of the rear wall of the shed to fall motionless to the floor. Stepping on a coal as she fitted the rods back into her hair once more, Kassandra looked at the men, "Are we ready to go now?"

In the short, but harrowing run to the storage building, Cobham saw that the gigantic *Windram* was now tied to a makeshift platform lashed to the backs of two of the leviathans. The men of the encampment were all focused on securing the dirigible but soon they would want to load it with the deadly cargo. Cobham knew they had little time and set to work on the latch with Kassandra's knife.

"Look," he whispered pointing upward. Dipping in and out among the massing storm clouds above was the brassy form of the *Sharpshin. Now we have a chance,* Cobham thought. If they could destroy the bombs and escape, then His Majesty's Aerofleet could deal with the *Windram.* The lock gave way under his hands and the door opened inward.

When Cobham glanced up again the *Sharpshin* was much closer. He could just make out the dangling form of the cargo lift. Their rescuers were on the way. Stepping into the dim interior he found himself standing among crates that filled the building to the rafters. He missed a breath, stunned.

"They're coming," Kassandra cried.

Cobham forced himself into motion. He grabbed the closest crate and handed it to Sparrowknife, then turned back to choose one from the floor. Hefting it to his shoulder he stepped outside of the storage building. A shot rang out and a fist-sized hole appeared in the icy exterior of the building next to him. "Run!" he cried, pushing Kassandra ahead of him toward the lowering cargo lift of the airship. Shots chuffed into the snow around them as they raced past their former prison and into the open. Cobham saw a streak of red in the snow but breathed a sigh of relief as he saw Sparrowknife stumble onto the cargo lift. A stray gust lifted the edge of the platform and Cobham slid the crate from his shoulder sending it skittering across the wood floor. Then he reached back to lift Kassandra up to Sparrowknife, who caught her. The cargo lift swayed as Cobham launched himself at it. The edge caught him in the stomach driving the air from him as he scrambled for purchase. The ropes sang, the whole lift shook as the *Sharpshin* lifted away.

Pellets shot from a blunderbuss scattered across the interior of the lift pinging like hail with most of its momentum spent. Sparrowknife, his left arm streaming with blood, elbow-walked his way across the platform until he could grasp Cobham with his good hand. Behind him, Kassandra clung to the airman's ankles. It took two tries but Cobham was able to swing his legs up over the siding of the lift. He lay there a moment gasping. Looking back over his shoulder, he could see the ground racing away from them. The *Sharpshin* drew closer as the winch brought up the cargo lift. Below, small forms raced toward the

Windram. Already he could see the gigantic dirigible turning as it was freed from its tie downs.

Could the airship outrun the dirigible? he wondered. More importantly, could they still destroy the stockpile of bombs and escape? As Kassandra stripped lining from her coat to create a makeshift bandage for Sparrowknife, Cobham crawled to the crate he'd brought aboard. When he threw open its latches, he let out an involuntary grunt of despair. Inside laid a weather balloon, packaged with a large coil of rope. Turning back to Sparrowknife he cried, "Dear Lord, I hope you have bombs in your crate." The airman pushed the other crate across the floor to Cobham. This time when the latches popped open there were three dark metal spheres nestled in wood shavings.

The light changed and Cobham looked up realizing that the *Sharpshin's* cargo bay was right above them. Their swaying decreased as the platform was swung to one side and the cargo bay doors began to close. Looking at Sparrowknife, Cobham cried out, "Don't let them close the doors. We have to drop the bombs on the store house."

"The captain will want to get out of here," Sparrowknife replied getting to his feet with Kassandra's help.

"Well you've got to convince him differently. If those bombs are used on the Aerofleet we won't stand a chance. Then imagine what a few of those could do if they were dropped on the His Majesty's Palace while you're at it. Just get Bornesun to make a pass low over the storage shed."

Sparrowknife looked grim, but he stumbled off toward the bridge. Already Cobham could feel the *Sharpshin* rising, attempting to gain altitude and the higher winds to try to out run the *Windram.*

Kassandra stepped up next to Cobham. "What can I do?" she asked.

"Moore said that the catalyst becomes active after an applied force. I assume he meant being fired from a cannon. Let's hope that force doesn't have to be very specific. Find me a bar, a hammer, any tool. I think it's time to apply some blunt force and hope we are very lucky."

They both looked about the interior of the cargo bay until Cobham found a large wrench. He reached into the crate to pull out one of the cannonball-sized spheres. Placing the bomb against the lip running about the edge of the cargo area, he rested his foot against its side. He swung the wrench over his head.

At the top of his arc, Kassandra asked, "Do you really think that is safe?"

Ignoring the question, Cobham brought the wrench down in a ringing blow on top of the iron sphere. They both turned and looked at each other for a second and then Cobham answered, "Has any of this been safe so far?" Setting down the wrench, he reached for the bomb. Lifting it with great care, he stepped up to the open maw of the cargo bay. Chilling wind blew his hair about. The *Sharpshin* was veering back. Something occurred to him so he turned back to the crate. Barely breathing, he restored the activated bomb to its nesting. Then in the remaining moments he struck each of the other spheres as well. Holding the third bomb in his hands, he leaned out over the opening. Behind him Kassandra knotted a hand through his braces, planting a foot against the back of each of his, leaning backward to anchor him in place. The ground came racing up as he dropped the heavy sphere over the side. Reaching for the second one, Cobham heaved it over as well.

The *Sharpshin* spun and they tumbled to the deck. The airship's nose tipped up as the craft raced for the heavens. As Cobham disentangled himself from Kassandra, he saw the crate bearing the remaining bomb sliding across the floor. Quick thinking as always, Kassandra shot out an arm, catching it before it could strike the lip at the edge of the cargo bay. Breathing a sigh of relief, Cobham crab-walked over to the crate. Taking a free length of rope, he lashed it to a tie-down near the open maw of the bay. Then Cobham turned and helped Kassandra to her feet. A flash lit up the sky behind them. Seconds later a rumble filled the enclosed space of the bay. Together they rushed to the edge of the opening to see the entire northern end of the encampment engulfed in flames. The roof of the storage shed fell downward in shards of metallic shrapnel. Continuing thumps sounded as the remaining bombs exploded. A final ear-shattering explosion followed, signaling the destruction of the oil reserve and the pump.

Turning back, Cobham found their view occluded. He blinked and when his eyes focused he realized he was looking at the broad nose of the *Windram* as it ascended toward them. Along its sides, he could see the blisters of the cannons swinging round to take aim. Sparrowknife came running into the bay skidding to a stop next to them, his eyes wide with horror at the sight coming toward them. Cobham reached down for the final sphere. *As large as the aeronaught is, could I miss?* he wondered. Taking the bomb in both hands, he leaned forward once more. This time both of his compatriots braced him. When the dirigible filled the whole of the bay, he let the bomb drop. As the sphere descended, two of the *Windram's* cannons fired, puffs of smoke drifting from the gunnery blisters. It almost felt like a race. *Will the bomb strike first or the cannon shot?* Cobham mused. Cannon shots streaked by the *Sharpshin*. The bomb, on the other hand, struck the aeronaught square on. Unfortunately, it merely dented the metallic skin of the dirigible and rolled off.

Cobham staggered back into his companions. He stumbled away from them to lean against the nearby steam harpoon gun. For a moment he weighed the possibility of firing the weapon at the aeronaught, *but what would one bolt do against the massive engine of destruction below them? It would be like pricking an elephant with a pin. What could they do now?* Perhaps he hadn't struck the bomb hard enough to prime it?

Sparrowknife leaned over him shaking Cobham's shoulder with his good arm. "Don't give up, old man. The captain's got more than a few tricks in him. Do you know why they have airships run guard duty on dirigibles? We're much more maneuverable and can take more hits than a rigid aircraft. If we lose a few cells, we shift them to regain balance. On the other hand, if the dirigible loses any cells it's no longer stable and becomes difficult to handle. Once its hull fails, it fails catastrophically."

"No, Airman, the only hand that counts right now is that the thing below is armored like a medieval castle."

"Not on top though," Kassandra offered.

"Doesn't matter...we've lost the only weapon any good against it," snapped Cobham.

A loud crack of thunder interrupted their argument as the *Sharpshin* altered course once again. "Well, there's another alternative. The captain is taking us up into the storm," Sparrowknife said, stepping closer to the bay. Behind the bulk of the *Windram* the horizon now churned an ominous bluish black. The light was fading from the sky.

Turning away from the image, Cobham caught sight of Kassandra's face. Her eyes were intent, focused on the aeronaught below. Her brow furrowed in thought. Just audible above the thunder she asked Sparrowknife, "Does the *Windram* look to you to have the same cladding as the downed dirigible?"

At first the airman was taken aback. Then he nodded. "If I had to guess then, yes. I would say it looks the same. It would make sense since the wreck was one of the Southron's."

"Then we have a chance. Constable get the other crate and bring it here. Airman is there any access to the gas cells here? We need to fill the weather balloon as quick as possible."

Not sure what Kassandra had in mind, Cobham pulled the lid off of the crate. He handed the folded package of the balloon to Sparrowknife. Taking out the rope Cobham swung back to Kassandra.

"We're going to need every length of rope here, Constable. Start tying them together." She reached out taking the end of the first coil of line from him. Then she stepped up to the steam harpoon. There she joined the length coiled at its base to the other, continuing to tie on each length of rope he found for her, pulling each knot tight. Finally, Kassandra tied the rope to the end of the harpoon load. She stepped back a moment surveying their work as Sparrowknife and several other airmen drug the large weather balloon into the bay.

"What are we doing, Kassandra?" Cobham asked now completely confused.

She looked past him through the open bay doors. The *Windram* rose below them once more. "Sparrowknife," she called, "how much do you think the captain trusts me? I need him to bring us close enough to the *Windram* that we can hit it with the harpoon gun."

"Why?"

"You gave me the answer earlier in the day. What can destroy a ship this size?"

The airman's eyes lit up with comprehension, "A lightning strike. A strike with the same cladding as the other ship had...." He took a deep breath. "Ye gods it could work. But we would have to be well away from the resulting explosion."

"That's why I'm thinking of something else you told me. We wait until they fire again. Then set loose a few of our gas cells to make them think we're hit. We can plunge past the *Windram,* fire the harpoon, play out the balloon and then get as far away as possible."

Sparrowknife called the other airmen over as he and Cobham took hold of the balloon. He gave them terse orders sending them off to the bridge and the upper tiers, respectively. "This crazy idea better work or I'm going to be grounded for good."

From the other side of the balloon, Cobham replied, "I think we'll all be under the ground in a permanent fashion if this doesn't work.

Kassandra joined them taking hold of the balloon. She tied the rope to its bottom and then tied the wrench that Cobham had used earlier several feet below the balloon. She grasped two fistfuls of the balloon fabric saying, "You'll need to make the shot, Sparrowknife. You're the expert here."

"I'm no expert at this craziness but at least you've given me a target that will be difficult to miss." The airman spun the locks open on the harpoon gun opening the steam valve to let the pressure build. Once again the *Sharpshin* bucked and spun. "That would be the cells away." The thunder was so loud now that they couldn't even hear their pursuer firing its guns.

Cobham and Kassandra struggled to maintain their grip on the weather balloon as it rippled and flexed under their hands. The surface of the *Windram* spun closer and closer. Cobham thought he could see the individual panels that made up the skin of the aeronaught. "Take the shot," he cried.

"Not yet," Sparrowknife screamed back over the rushing wind.

Now Cobham could see the rivets holding the cladding down. *Surely, the cannons have a bead on us by now,* he thought. As he was waiting for the inevitable shudder from the impact, Kassandra cried, "Let go!"

Confused, Cobham maintained his grip on the balloon as it surged, sucked downward as the *Sharpshin* rolled. When Sparrowknife at last fired the harpoon, a cloud of steam filled the bay for a second before being sucked out. The bolt arrowed downward to disappear into the skin of the *Windram*. Cobham slid across the floor with the gasbag, letting go at the edge of the bay. For a moment, the balloon hung there in the opening. Then it was gone and the rope sang over the edge, coil after coil unfurling.

"Hold on," Sparrowknife sang out as the *Sharpshin* dove toward its foe. The airship skimmed well between the outthrust spars of the aeronaught's giant fans to continue its plunge toward the sea below. The cargo bay doors swung ponderously closed. As the airship picked up speed, Cobham heard the whine of the ship's own fans cranking well past their safety limits. He could feel a slight change in their angle. The fans were going so fast now that the entirety of the *Sharpshin* shook in sympathetic vibration. As the airship leveled out, Sparrowknife gestured them all toward the bridge. They raced through the hallways being battered against the sides as the ship shuddered onward. Cobham burst out on the decking behind the others as Captain Bornesun set the fans to freewheeling, letting them cycle down. As rough wind continued to buffet the airship, they all found themselves clutching the brass railing as the captain brought the *Sharpshin* around.

"What now, captain?" asked Sparrowknife.

"If your crazy scheme doesn't work we're going to ram them. There is no way I am letting that ship return to its home port."

There was a moment of quiet as they turned to watch the cloud deck above them. The *Sharpshin* had dropped low enough that the waters of the North Atlantic rippled not far beneath the ship. From the black cloud emerged the prow of the *Windram*. Their ploy was unsuccessful. The aeronaught pulled a full third of its length through the clouds angling toward them.

Bornesun leveled out their course aiming the *Sharpshin's* prow at the *Windram*. The captain reached down for the fan gear shaft, preparing to ram the aeronaught. A flash lit up the cloud deck as an immense arc of electricity flung itself from cloud to cloud. It branched like a fiery tree. The skin of the *Windram* glowed with blue luminosity for an instant. Then the entire front of the aeronaught dissolved into a billowing cascade of fire. Orange and reddish light lit up the horizon. As more and more of the dirigible fell below the layer of cloud, further explosions rocked the skies. Shredded wreckage drifted down over the ocean like a charred snowfall. Still the immense ship fell. Gas cells burst from the framework to detonate into incandescent flares. The prow reached the water level as the entire pillar of radiance collapsed under its own weight. The sound wave struck the *Sharpshin* and the airship shuddered under the violence of the *Windram's* passing. Bornesun silently crossed himself and set to turning the airship away.

"I wonder what happened to Cyrus the ghost," Sparrowknife asked.

"I suspect that destroying the expedition and doing in Moore probably set things to rights for him," Kassandra said in a dull monotone.

Looking away from the wreck of the *Windram*, at Kassandra, Cobham found her lips set in a hard line. "We've done good today, Constable. Even though we had to fight them on their own terms," she stated. The light of the burning pyre caught the glass pins in her hair, the shine in her eyes of unshed tears.

We've done good, he thought. Perhaps they had. Perhaps that was what he was meant to do. He could do it one person at a time on the streets of Amphyra or perhaps he was meant for more. Cobham was certain of one thing; he'd never felt as alive as he had in the last few hours. It could be that was his reward for doing the right thing. If that was the case, then sticking by Kassandra's side was the right decision. "Thanks for the excitement," he said quietly. She chuckled and laid a hand over his for a moment. Then she turned to walk down the stairs to the crew quarters.

Sparrowknife tipped his head to one side. "You know, I never saw Moore board the *Windram.*"

"I didn't either. I'm certain she knows it as well, but we should let that be for the moment."

Both men turned back to look at the fading light from the wreck of the aeronaught as it fell into the distance. The storm rolled over the blazing remains, obscuring them from view. For now Cobham was content to be headed home. He knew he'd chosen a dangerous path, but now there was a certainty that he'd often seemed to lack, a confirmation that he'd chosen the right one.

Now Fear This

THE RATTLE OF THE BOAT'S FAN MOTOR CUT OFF COBHAM'S COMMENT. Kassandra turned to him. "What was that, Constable?"

"Nothing I should repeat in front of a lady, more than likely." He hefted the oar Padraigh had given him to push off from the docks, considering where to stow it. The Irishman leaned on the lever and the boat lurched forward, creating a wave of greenish black water. Cobham tucked the oar to one side of the bench at the center of the craft where Kassandra was seated. The medium clutched her hat to her head and leaned into the wind, her other arm threaded through the bar in front of the seat. Cobham guessed if one spoke to the dead regularly and dealt with the strangeness of the supernatural, then some wind and water were not of great import. Sliding in next to her, he watched Padraigh steer the boat, his arms working the levers and feet moving on the control treadles. As they rounded the end of the channel, the wind came up behind them blowing the smoke from steam boilers back through the large fans, making them all cough.

"You're grinding your teeth, Constable."

"And despite how many times you remind me of it, I still continue."

"Really, whatever is the matter?"

Cobham turned to her, looking Kassandra square in her blue eyes and stated, "Put me on a street with a group of thugs, drunkards, or whatever you like and I shall do fine. Someone who walks the cobbles doesn't belong on the water."

"And I have more reason to be here? The Director of the Royal Security Division isn't someone to be trifled with, so when he says "You two will be investigating deaths at the Delta Listening Posts", it's not as though we had a choice."

Cobham turned away, mumbling under his breath, hoping that the wind might cover his response.

"Well, I know I'm here to speak to those that died; as for you, perhaps you will feel more at home thumping criminals on their heads." Kassandra brushed her red curls back away from her face.

When she wavered, as the boat struck the first of the waves from coming in from the Gulf, Cobham put out a hand and steadied her. "I'm here to see that you come back in one piece." Padraigh, on the other hand, seemed to have little concern for his passengers. Cobham found himself grinning briefly at the thought of the little rotund man turning around at their destination to discover their bench empty. As they moved further away from the port of Amphyra into the waters at the mouth of the Delta, the ride grew rougher as the boat pitched forward and back. Padraigh turned the prow of the boat toward a dark mass on the horizon and they plowed onward. Cobham could see a dock as they rounded the curve of the island. The rickety wooden structure jutted out into the turbulent water. Padraigh brought them around it, choosing to fetch the boat up against the long portion that ran parallel to the shoreline.

Carefully maneuvering the fans, Padraigh kept the boat in place until Cobham leapt to the dock and lashed the ropes located fore and aft to the cleats there. Then he reached out and steadied Kassandra as she stepped ashore. As Padraigh trimmed the boil on the furnace driving the steam engine, Cobham glanced about their surroundings. Just up the beach stood a round building, with a series of strange protrusions from the roof. It looked for all the world as if someone had mounted the brass section of an orchestra upon the top of the structure.

There was a raised walkway that ran to the building, which itself stood on stilts well above the dunes. Considering the weather in the delta, it made sense to raise a structure up above any potential flooding.

A movement in the reeds along the path leading to the building caught Cobham's eye. He leaned back into the boat for a moment and reclaimed the oar. Bracing himself on it, he pulled out his revolver and made sure each of its three barrels was primed and loaded. Then he shoved it back into its holster. A good constable only used his weapon as a last resort and besides swinging a truncheon was usually a bit more pleasant than having to spend the time reloading. Of course his truncheon was at the station house, so he'd have to make due with an oar. *No sense in being unprepared,* he thought.

Cobham took the lead and started up the path. Padraigh was helping Kassandra up onto the steps from the beach when an alligator came charging out of the reeds at them. Cobham did not hesitate and shoved the narrow paddle straight into the creature's open maw. He turned it before the creature could draw its mouth closed and shoved the paddle as far forward as he could, propping open the creature's jaws. The gator thrashed about wildly as Cobham continued to push, making it slowly retreat. Eventually, the reptile grew tired of the game, its teeth grinding against the lacquer on the wood. It threw its head about, nearly wrenching the oar from Cobham's hand. The gator then stared at him and his drawn gun for a moment before turning to lunge into the reeds.

Kassandra looked back at him from the raised walkway. At least Padraigh had the good sense to get her out of the way. Cobham hefted the oar for a moment before joining them.

"That one seemed pretty frisky," Kassandra observed.

Cobham turned and made a point of latching the gate on the walkway. "True."

He considered the building ahead of them. It wasn't the only thing strange around here. He gestured them aside with the hand not holding the gun and, passing on the narrow walkway, took the lead. He was only vaguely familiar with the Listening Post program. Cobham knew that the peculiar collection of horns on the roof of the building were capable of concentrating the sound from miles around. The soldiers stationed here were responsible for identifying Southron dirigibles and airships that might try to sneak across the border into New Britain. The soldiers would then warn the guards on the coast via signal rocket and heliograph.

The men on duty here were trained to pick out the sounds of engines and turbines from the cries of gulls and the surf. Their training took a long time and few had sharp enough senses to complete the course. That made them valuable assets. According to the reports from the Directorate, there had been four deaths so far, all under mysterious circumstances. That left only two listeners running the station until more could be brought in from other locations. Cobham and Kassandra had been dispatched to investigate before any others fell victim.

When they reached the wide porch that encircled the building, Padraigh picked a bench and dropped heavily on it. "I'll leave you to it."

Cobham considered him for a moment. He couldn't help but notice the distance the man had kept between himself and Kassandra. The Irishman might have ferried them here but he'd no desire to become involved in the supernatural aspects of their endeavor. Cobham shrugged and handed the oar to him. "Thanks for getting us here, Paddy. I'll stand you a pint when we get back."

"Well, sure. I could hardly say no." With that he leaned back and tipped his cap down over his eyes.

Cobham looked about. Well, the swamp denizens were not going to get to the boatman here. Paddy firmly disbelieved in ghosts, so none should bother him. The constable felt a shiver run up his spine, Cobham on the other hand knew better. If one wasn't careful, the unnatural could cause all kinds of trouble.

Kassandra rolled her eyes at Paddy and pulled open the door to the station before Cobham could protest. He followed her into the whitewashed interior. *This must be a cloakroom,* he thought as he noted several oilskins hung along the wall with pairs of boots arranged beneath them. The rough carpeting on the floor muffled their steps but seemed out of place, given the nature of the room. Of course, there would be measures to avoid random sounds that might interfere with the listening devices. Kassandra nodded to him, after noticing his glance, and placed a finger to her lips. They should do their best not to interrupt the function of the post. Before she could preempt his move, Cobham stepped to the next door and pulled it open.

This led to a short hallway. The first threshold opened up into the dining room. A lone figure sat at a table with his back to them. A heavy scarf was wrapped like a turban around his head and over his ears. Cobham found it bizarre but he remembered being warned that the men stationed here were not exactly run-of-the-mill soldiers. This particular conscript ate fishy smelling chowder as he paged his way through a book, blissfully unaware of their presence.

When Kassandra stepped into his field of view, he dropped his spoon with a loud clatter and sent his bowl spinning noisily away from his hands. Realizing what he'd done, he froze like a rabbit, his gray eyes round. Cobham reached out and stilled the bowl.

The constable watched as the other man stood carefully and backed away from the stool he'd occupied. He gestured come hither and then led them from the dining room back to the hallway. They padded along after him, the carpet absorbing their footfalls. At the end of the corridor, the way forked and at the join stood a door surmounted by a porthole and sealed by a wheel lock.

Their guide turned to the left and as they continued, Cobham realized they were moving about the center of the complex. The hub must be the seat where the listeners filtered through the focused sound gathered by the array of horns. At the next corner they turned left down another corridor. At the end, a second door opened out onto the porch once again. There the listener turned and facing them threw out his hands palms up, looking back and forth between them.

Cobham opened his mouth, but Kassandra put a finger to his lips, then leaned forward to catch the end of the scarf. She pulled down and ripped it from the young man's head in one swift motion. Apparently, she'd reached the end of her patience. "Did no one tell you we were coming?"

The other visibly flinched, drawing back from her vehemence. His eyes darted about and he gasped until Kassandra flailed at him with the scarf.

"Stop that!" he squeaked in a singularly petulant voice. "How could I know you were coming? I'm dreadful at heliograph and because Caine is occupied in the chamber there's no one else to watch."

That left Cobham confused. "So what do you do if there is a sighting?"

"I fire the signal rocket." He looked at them as if they were mad. "And actually it's called a sounding, if an airship is identified." That last came across in a haughty tone as he crossed his arms. Kassandra rolled her eyes and then threw a hand across them.

Cobham had come to the end of his rope as well. He mustered the tone that always worked on young recruits, "Well, sound this, soldier. I am Constable Cobham Peckwith and this is Madam Kassandra Leyden and we are here to find out why your comrades are dead. It might occur to you that would also mean we're one of the best chances you have of getting off of this sand heap alive."

The young man rocked backward as if struck. He straightened his back and his heels snapped together. Cobham nodded. That was more like it. "What's your name, soldier?"

"Listener Guildeford, sir."

Nodding, Cobham strode up to Guildeford and, putting a hand on his shoulder, led him to one of the porch benches. He pushed him down brusquely and squatted down on his haunches before the soldier, pushing back his cap. "Why don't you tell us what's happened here, son?" Kassandra strode up to stand at Cobham's shoulder to listen.

"There were six of us," began Guildeford looking down at his shoes, unwilling to meet Cobham or Kassandra's gaze. "That's our normal complement. Enough that we could run three shifts in pairs or do single shifts if someone got sick. We're typically stationed here a month at a time with a week's leave after that and rotated out as necessary to other stations. There were a few false alarms and two crossing attempts. It wasn't until Hastings actually managed to shoot down the one airship that things got out of hand."

"Hastings shot the signal rocket at an airship?" Kassandra was obviously stunned and Cobham felt the same.

"That's a foolhardy move," he commented and then gestured to Guildeford to continue.

"No one's ever said we couldn't. It was just that no one really expected it to work either. The rocket ruptured the main air bag of the ship and then proceeded to catch the frame on fire. It went up like a paper lantern. It was rather amazing."

"I'm sure the Southrons didn't feel that way about it," Kassandra interrupted, crossing her arms over her chest. She certainly looked unhappy with the way the questioning was going.

"The next morning Hastings was dead. He'd fallen over the railing there and broken his neck. We barely found him before the gators did. At first we thought it was an accident. Then at lunch, Avery pitched over into the soup cooking away on the stove, which was a shame, because it had been one of the better chowders that Caine had made. After we got him cleaned up, we couldn't find any cause of death. Pell died in the shower the next day. We found her blood running down the drain. She'd been stabbed in the back of the leg. Wittershin was the most recent fatality. He'd managed to get the signal rocket set up to let the mainland know we were in serious trouble and then someone stuck a screwdriver into his ear. We found him sprawled over the rocket. Caine and I got him down and fired it off and now here you are."

"What did you do with the bodies?"

Guildeford swung around and stared a Kassandra. It clearly wasn't the question he'd been expecting. Cobham on the other hand wasn't surprised at all.

"We put them in the springhouse. It's around the other side of the building. The ground water level is very high here and it keeps a sealed room cool."

Cobham pulled himself back up to his feet. "Perhaps, you should introduce us to Listener Caine."

Guildeford nodded and when he got up, Kassandra stopped him with a hand clasped to his arm. "Has Listener Caine been able to hear us the whole time?"

"You mean you can't hear it? The dampner? There's a device that layers this entire area in interference, which cancels out incidental sounds. Caine would have heard your boat arrive, but couldn't have heard anything around the post itself. The dampner would feel like a low hum to you. May setting your teeth on edge? Wittershin made it. He was rather a genius with sound, always tinkering around with bits and bobs of this and that. It annoyed the hell of him that he always had to tune out external sounds when he was listening. Besides it finally gave us some place where we could actually talk. We're already an odd lot here but being silent all the time was driving us barmy. The dampner masks everything inside except the listening chamber and even extends over the post and some of the grounds. The officer who'd stopped by a week ago was fascinated by it. Thought that all of the stations should have one.

"Anyway, Caine can't hear us here due to that. We're just quiet by nature inside, because we don't want to harm each other's hearing. Well, I should say we were." He looked wistfully out over the sand for a moment and then, gesturing for them to follow, led Cobham and Kassandra back into the building.

This time they made their way to the center. Cobham almost ran into Guildeford as he came to a sudden stop in front of a door with a heavy baffle about it, the frame layered in fabric forming a seal to minimize the amount of incidental noise. Guildeford spun the wheel lock around and then led them over the threshold.

Cobham was surprised to discover that the chamber had a glass roof. Through the dome of clear panels, he could see the immense copper, flower-shaped tubes of the sonic collectors. Each of the tubes faced a different direction and layers of them built up into a mound overhead. Bellowed connectors brought everything together into a single brass cylinder that descended above a couch-like chair. Listener Caine sat there, hands on the armrests, feet dangling off the end of the couch, her golden-haired head leaned back into an open hemisphere that Cobham assumed was the terminus of all of the equipment gathered overhead. Her eyes popped open and then she was pushing herself up out of the seat, her lips parted in surprise.

"Caine, this is Constable Peckwith and Madam Leyden. They are here—"

"To investigate the deaths of course. Don't be a dolt, Guildeford. This is hardly the spot for a sightseeing destination." Caine was of a height similar to Kassandra, a bit shorter than himself, and Cobham found her grip strong as he shook her hand. Her hair was pulled back into a tight knot at the nape of her neck and she wore the same sand-colored uniform as Guildeford: tunic, jodhpurs and a shiny pair of boots.

"Perhaps you should see where we found the bodies and where we are keeping them." She indicated the door on the far side of the chamber and led them to it. There was a brief awkward moment, when Guildeford stood behind them at the doorway until Caine gave him a sharp glance and he retreated to the couch, settling himself into position. Cobham caught Kassandra's amused glance and nod.

The listener led them through another soundproof door, across the hallway and to a window. She indicated a small building visible below the walkway. "There's the springhouse." A gator walked slowly through the grass just outside of the fenced-in area that contained the outbuilding.

"Have you been having trouble with the alligators?" Cobham asked.

Hand on the sill, Caine commented, "It's odd. They've been strangely aggressive recently." She pointed with her other hand, indicating the fence. "We put this up because they were a nuisance and lately I've been glad we did."

Caine said, "Constable, I understand why you are here, but I'm not certain why the heliograph said they were sending a medium. I hear a lot of strange things doing my job, but I've never heard, much less seen a spirit."

Cobham cast Kassandra a glance, but it seemed she was going to be kind.

"Just because you can't see it doesn't mean it doesn't exist. As you've been trained to use your extraordinary hearing, I've been training to listen as well. It does however turn out that the dead don't speak, at least not in the way you'd expect. With me,

they do tend to find a way to get their point across though."
Kassandra smiled at Caine and then turned to stare intently out
the window. "What's that then?" she asked, gesturing toward a
black structure that lay among the stunted trees just past the
springhouse.

"That's the burnt frame of the Southron airship."

With that, clearly assuming they were finished here, Caine
turned to lead them down the hallway.

Kassandra shot out a hand and caught Cobham's arm.
"Constable, there's something horribly wrong here," she
whispered. "I can't find any of their spirits. In fact I can't hear
anything from any spirit. People like this who died as they did
at their tasks, would more than likely leave behind some sort
of remnant, at least for a while. They died with their work in-
complete."

"You mean there are no ghosts about?" he asked and then
cast a glance back toward Caine, who had moved several
steps away. "What if being out here by themselves and forced
to listen for something they could barely hear finally drove
one of these two over the edge? Guildeford seems plenty
twitchy."

Kassandra's expression tightened. "I can't disprove, nor prove
your theory, Constable. You are however correct about one thing.
When a spirit doesn't immediately move on as it should, it is generally referred to as a ghost. It certainly wouldn't be surprising
to have something like that occur here. In fact, the crew of that
crashed airship might also have become agitated spirits because
they were abruptly stopped in their task. It's strange that I can
perceive none of them. Something is happening here and I can't
explain it yet. I think Caine is right. Let's investigate where the
deaths happened."

As the listener led them into the dining room, a knife came
sailing through the air at Caine. Before he could think about
what he was seeing, Cobham shouldered her out of its path.
Doing so, he struck something he couldn't see. He felt the weight
behind the invisible obstacle and pushed it aside. The knife
came to a halt in mid air, swung about and returned stabbing
downward at Cobham. He threw up an arm hoping to deflect it,
his wrist striking toward the handle. Instead of impacting the

weapon, he hit something else. It almost felt like a hand. At this point his instinct took over and he kicked out, connecting solidly. The knife clattered to the floor and spun away. Caine scooped it up.

Throwing out his arms, Cobham flailed about until he felt his adversary. That unfortunately meant they had a chance to swing at him. He felt a blow hit his ribs before his hands came down on the other's shoulders. Guessing at their location, he brought up his knee feeling it connect with what he hoped was the other's jaw. Cobham shoved his opponent away from him and the invisible form struck the closest table shoving it backward across the floor. Then Cobham turned to run. "Get out!" he cried.

Fortunately, Kassandra and Caine had already come to the same conclusion and were fleeing through the doorway ahead of him. As he passed through the entrance, a chair struck the wall beside the frame and shattered into pieces. Cobham fumbled for the door and slammed it shut as a heavy impact hit the wood. Taking one of the pieces of the chair, he shoved the sheared-off end under the bottom of the door to wedge it shut.

Hands on his knees he stood there for a moment, panting heavily. When he brought his head up, he looked at Kassandra and said wryly, "I think I found one of your ghosts."

Her expression was grim. "I think it's not that simple, Constable. There were other objects moving in the room during your fight. Two of the doors opened on their own. I'm afraid that it's not just one of the ghosts from the Southron airship, there were other spirits here as well."

"So we're trapped here with the dead crew of a crashed airship who've suddenly found a way to touch the living?"

"Not exactly. I'm afraid we're trapped here with a group of vengeful ghosts who've found a way to kill the living." As that statement hung in the air, Kassandra turned to Caine. "Listener, you're bleeding."

As Cobham straightened up, Kassandra examined the gash on the other woman's arm. The medium tore off the damaged sleeve from Caine's blouse to bind the wound, caused by a flying piece of chair from the fight. "How long do you think we have before they find us again?" asked Cobham as he looked down the corridor.

"They'll have to go out the back of the kitchen and around. So we have some time," Caine answered, tugging her tunic back on.

"Unless they weren't all in the dining room to begin with," opined Kassandra as she dug in the pocket of her jacket. She pulled out two amber hair sticks with a smile, "I do have an idea though that might help us. It would certainly give us an advantage, if we could see them. I couldn't see the point of trying to keep these in my hair with all of that wind, but they do come in handy." She began to rapidly rub the hair sticks across the surface of her wool skirt, until the fibers began to stand up with each pass.

"Planning on stabbing ghosts with those?" Caine asked skeptically.

"I suspect it will be a lot stranger than that," Cobham replied.

"Indeed," Kassandra said as she put the rods on either side of her forehead and small blue sparks leapt from their ends to her skin.

Cobham watched Kassandra's eyes roll briefly up into her head and then she recovered, staggering slightly. He moved forward and placed a hand at her elbow to steady her. When Kassandra opened her mouth a graceful, web-like mist of silvery ectoplasm emerged. She quickly gathered it up and then breathed forth more. After a pool of it gathered in her palm, quaking with each of her motions, she dipped a finger into the silver and then swiftly applied it to her right eye. She wobbled once again, and he gripped her more firmly until she turned back to him, suddenly smiling. Her countenance was now unearthly, one eye a silver orb and the other her familiar blue.

Caine stood there gasping like a fish. Kassandra turned her unearthly gaze toward the woman. "Listener, there's always something strange out there beyond our little comfortable norms. Today that's me and my ability to speak to the dead." She spun the pool of ectoplasm about in her palm. "And that's not all I can do." Caine's jaw snapped closed and she gave Kassandra a sharp nod. Then the medium closed one eye after the other and then finally turned to him. "Your turn, Constable."

As she dropped the film of ectoplasm over his eye, Cobham felt a frisson of icy cold. Like Kassandra, he stumbled trying to find his balance. He kept the eye veiled in ectoplasm covered until he once again found his feet. When he cautiously opened it, Cobham found it necessary to close his other eye because both images were so incongruous. Looking through the ectoplasm, the corridor was a dimly lit passage and the brightest objects were his companions. Each of them shone with a silvery light that radiated off of them in long diffused waves. His own hand held before him was a fiery blaze. Cobham opened his other eye and after a moment or two was able to slowly stabilize himself, his mind taking in both worlds and layering the images one over the other.

"Constable," hissed Kassandra pointing a finger down the hallway. Then he noticed the shadow moving toward them.

The ghost, unlike Kassandra or Caine, did not radiate the silvery light, but rather sucked it in. All of the strange waves he was seeing streamed and ran toward the shadowy figure as though it were a hole sucking down the illumination. He reached out for his companions and pushed them ahead of him. "They're here." As the ladies began to run down the corridor, he cursed himself for not taking another instant to consider their destination. Now they were heading away from the listening chamber and toward the cloakroom where they had entered the post.

When they skidded through the doorway, Cobham looked about the room seeking any kind of weapon. He wasn't certain what he could use on a vengeful spirit or even *if* he could harm a ghost.

As Kassandra slammed the door to the cloakroom shut and slid the room's one chair under the doorknob, Caine asked, "If these are the ghosts of the Southron crew, then where are the ghosts of my compatriots?"

Cobham looked at Kassandra and found her considering the question.

"They're probably locked inside the springhouse. They are more recently deceased and may not be as adjusted to their state as the spirits from the airship. They may not realize they can lay a hand on things and move them yet. However, one spirit can touch another. They could be the only way to overcome our adversaries," Kassandra stated. At her back a measured thumping began as the door started to jump in its frame.

"Persistent devils," said Cobham grimly as he opened the door to the walkway circumscribing the post. Caine pointed the way and he closed one eye after another in an attempt to discern if any of their enemies were before them. The way was clear and they set off. In the back of his mind, Cobham was glad they were moving away from the other side of the building where they'd left Paddy asleep on the bench. If they'd any luck, he'd still be around to ferry them back after all of this. As their feet rung on the wooden planking, he glanced back to make sure Kassandra was keeping up. Behind them a window shattered and a dark figure began to emerge through the gap. The chase was on once more.

When they at last reached the stairway that led down to the springhouse, Cobham spied another dark figure ahead of him. This time he didn't hesitate. He could see his opponent and there was no point in not charging in. Lowering his shoulder, he slammed into the ghost, plowing it into the railing. He kept pushing until he forced the other away from the entrance to the stairs. They struggled on the wooden planking, each trying to force the other off balance, but it was Cobham who finally succeeded. He kicked the other in their barely visible shin and then snapped their other foot from under them. His adversary fell against the railing. Reaching out, Cobham levered them up and over, making sure they fell outside of the fencing. He briefly wondered if the gators would notice a ghost in their midst. Had he even hurt his adversary? There was no way to tell, but the path was now clear.

He headed down the stairs toward the small lawn surrounding the springhouse. Kassandra had made her way to the outbuilding and unlatched the door. Already he could see other figures gathering about her. These apparitions were not aggressive. They had found their allies and perhaps not a moment too soon. The light-swallowing forms of the dead airship men were running toward them down the walkway. Kassandra spoke rapidly to the four deceased listeners and then they broke away from her, fanning out in front of the living to shield them.

Watching all of this and preparing himself once again to fight, Cobham considered their odds. There were seven dark figures advancing on them. Even if they were to overcome them, could the spirits be bound? Could they lock *them* in the springhouse?

It was Kassandra who asked the question he should have awhile ago. "Constable, why can they touch us?"

"What else doesn't fit?" he asked in response and then answered his own question, "alligators."

"Caine when did the gators start becoming so aggressive?"

"About two weeks ago," she replied quickly.

"Maybe about the same time the dampner was turned on?"

"That's it, Constable," Kassandra said. "The dampner. Somehow it doesn't just dampen sound, it causes interference in the bodies of the departed. It changes their phase and allows them to touch things physically. It must also be something the alligators can hear and is making them upset."

"Got it. Stop the dampner, stop the ghosts." Cobham set his jaw and turned back to the fight. "First, we have to get past them."

"Not exactly," interrupted Caine as she pointed under the struts holding up the listening post. "The dampner is in the listening room, which is at the center of the post. Underneath the center is a staircase that leads up to the room. It's how they brought all of the equipment inside."

"Nothing between there and here except an unknowable amount of gators," mused Cobham.

Then Caine was already moving toward the fence. "I can at least see the gators." She put one foot against the wood slating and pushed. After several tries the enclosure splintered and a section fell forward. Because it was only waist high and served primarily as a visual deterrent, the fence wasn't exceptionally strong. She and Cobham armed themselves with the longest pieces of wood that came free. Swinging it about a few times to get the feel of it, Cobham grinned. Not exactly a truncheon, but it would do. Looking back, Cobham gestured to Kassandra to follow them. She hesitated for a moment and then realized that despite their valiant efforts, the defending spirits they'd left behind could only hold the stairway for so long. Then they were off and running into the twilight beneath the post.

The first gator came from the left and Cobham missed it. The reptile lunged for Kassandra and succeeded in sinking its teeth into her skirt. It gave a convulsive shake of its head and tore a chunk out of the fabric. In the meantime, Caine struck it soundly across the eyes with her stave. It thrashed away and promptly ended up in the path of the next gator. Accepting the good luck for what it was, they ran on.

Cobham could see the steps materializing out of the gloom when the next reptile lunged for him. He actually felt the teeth slide across the top of his boot as he dragged his foot aside without a second to spare. He plunged the sharp end of his fence post toward the gator. It struck the scaly head and bounced away. He backpedaled furiously, barely keeping his balance. The beast swung its head about seeking its prey and those few precious moments brought Cobham close to the bottom of the stairs. Happily the ladies were already on their way upward. Then the gator shot forward, after him again.

Cobham gave in and pulled his gun. He kept retreating until his heel struck the lowest step. Awkwardly, Cobham tried to gauge how much he needed to lift his foot while focusing on his reptilian nemesis. It watched him warily; just outside of the circle of light that formed when Caine threw open the hatch into the listening chamber. He could almost sense the consideration going on inside that wedge-shaped head. What was truly strange was that when he looked at it with his ectoplasm-covered eye, there was something there not unlike the apparitions he'd struggled with earlier. Did alligators have spirits?

Perhaps that moment of introspection was his mistake. Cobham stepped up onto the first riser and then hopped onto the second. In that moment, the beast lunged at him, trapping his left foot into its maw. The pain was exceptional, its teeth piercing but somewhat resisted by the heavy leather of his boots. He fell back against the steps, by some miracle managing to keep hold of his gun. When he brought the weapon around and fired, the gator shook its head, causing the shot to graze the thick skin above its right eye.

Panting in agony, Cobham struggled to roll the barrel of the revolver about and pull back on the hammer, praying there was still enough powder adhering to the pan. His head fell back and he could see that overhead, Kassandra was pulling at a mass of wires that entered the top of a gold cylinder behind the listening chair. Without considering the consequences, he brought up the gun and aimed. But instead of the bullet tearing through the skull of the reptile that had his foot in its mouth, it passed through the delicate machinery of what he could only assume was the dampening mechanism.

Reflex had him rolling the barrel of the gun once more, bringing the final shot into play. But it wasn't necessary. The gator had stopped its thrashing, disgorged his foot, and then slid down the lowest stair to lie there in the half light. It gave a sudden shiver along its whole body and then turned about to vanish into the darker reaches beneath the listening post. Cobham let the gun fall to one side and rest on one of the stairway's risers. When he blearily looked upward, Kassandra's head peered through the hatch framed by a halo of her red curls. Guildeford's moon-faced expression of shock was right next to her. Then Cobham passed out.

✠

He woke with a start, realizing he was laid out on a bench on the listening post's walk way. Cobham's ankle pulsed with a dull thump of pain and he could see his boot lying on the wooden planking, its leather perforated by holes. His stocking, caked with blood, had been pulled over a bulky bandage. He blinked. The ectoplasm was gone and he could see normally. Someone nudged him and offered a silver flask. He took it and accepted a swallow of something fiery but surprisingly smooth. Glaring owlishly at Paddy, Cobham pulled himself backward onto an armrest. The action provoked his ankle and a fresh flood of pain rushed over him. He tossed the flask of hooch back to the boatman.

"That woman owes me a refill. She used a lot on you. Said it was for 'medicinal purposes'. Like that's not what I use it for, *hunh*." With that Paddy took another long swallow.

It came slowly to Cobham that perhaps it was best that their pilot not finish all of the contents. He gestured for Paddy to return the flask. It flew back to him and Cobham had another sip and then tucked it away in his jacket. Paddy snorted at him and made a rude gesture. Something else occurred to Cobham. "You slept through the whole thing didn't you?"

Paddy glared at him. "T'wasn't easy. You lot made quite a racket."

That at least made Cobham laugh, which in turn made him flinch in pain.

The Irishman leaned over and handed Cobham something strung on a piece of cord. It was a large alligator tooth. "She said you'd want that. She also did a nice job of stitching you up as well. Fine woman, 'xcept for stealing my drink." He then proceeded to pull his hat over his eyes and lean backward. "Just wake me when you're ready to go."

Cobham fumbled the tooth around in his hand. He imagined that Kassandra was perhaps seeing to the spirits of the departed now that they were no longer dangerous. He hoped that she'd be able to give them some sort of peace. Then they could return to Amphyra and normalcy. That made him laugh again, *normalcy*. He hadn't had any of that since he'd met her. A moment later, he realized that writing up the report of today's activities was going to be quite a task. As quietly as possible, he pulled out Paddy's flask and had another sip. Best take his medicine now while he could.

CHASING ANUBIS

ENTERING THE CONCOURSE BELOW THE AIRSHIP QUAY, KASSANDRA Leyden felt she was ready for Londinium, but wished she were more confident about the task ahead. She'd put her goggles on before leaving the dirigible and settled a cloth mask over her mouth, protection against the contaminated air, full of the fumes of burning coal. She had learned the hard way on her first visit that the haze stung unshielded eyes and made them tear. The echo of her steps chased themselves across the empty tiled area. She'd come in on the latest arriving flight and the hustle and bustle of the day had moved on to the parlors, bawdy houses and other entertainments, now that the working hours were done. A lone chestnut seller cried his wares at the edge of the street. She sighed, taking in a chill breath of winter air.

A single black lorry waited just before the chestnut vendor. It bore red and gold lamps. She didn't need to see the door from here to know that it was embossed with the seal of the Directorate. Kassandra came to a halt at the curb and hesitated. She'd been told there were deaths involved with unusual artifacts and that she was sent to investigate as only her ability to speak to spirits would allow. But the details were meager.

She wished that Cobham was here with her. Kassandra had grown accustomed to the constable's presence on her recent adventures. However, he'd been placed in charge of a new group of recruits and couldn't break away on such short notice. The constable had presented her with a traveling gift. Pressing down on the stiletto's length at her side, hidden under her fur-lined coat, she was reassured.

The cab driver clambering down from his perch interrupted Kassandra's thoughts. He took her luggage and secured it to the rear of the carriage, then offered a white-gloved hand to help her up the step into its gloomy interior. Inside, she removed her goggles and mask. A single lamp, dimmed by a scarlet shroud, swung overhead. The light wobbled as the cab rolled forward, illuminating a man seated across from her, lounging against the side of the coach. He regarded her under dark brows, skin like stained mahogany, his thin graying hair draped across his balding head. Then he leaned forward, grinning madly. "Madam Leyden, it is such an absolute pleasure to meet you. I am a great fan of the exploits of your family and, of course, of your recent forays into the field, as well. I've read all of your father's books. I can't imagine what it must have been like to grow up in such a house.

"But, I am remiss, allow me to introduce myself, I am Samir Alhambra, antiquities expert. Also, this is my wife, Lady Eileena Alhambra."

Eileena came forth like a shade, her form coalescing out of the darkened interior. She wore a red satin dress and a red headscarf. In the tinted light of the carriage, she'd vanished. Dark eyes and brows of a similar nature to her husband rested above her delicate nose and a scarlet set of full lips. While her husband struck Kassandra as being of Middle Eastern descent, Eileena's background seemed grounded in the Mediterranean. Her teeth flashed briefly, as she reached for Kassandra's hand. She had a strong grip and Kassandra gave back as good as she got until Eileena broke off the clutch. "A pleasure to meet another strong and sure woman," Eileena said nodding her head at Kassandra, who returned the gesture and then placed her hands in her lap, hoping this might signal her hosts to proceed.

Samir broke in, "I hope you do not mind if we begin immediately. There is an auction tonight and once we realized the time of your flight, the best plan was to catch you upon arrival and head directly there. Have you had a chance to review the information the Directorate sent?"

"Certainly," responded Kassandra as she settled back into the cushions. "There's been an influx of artifacts recently that do not have established histories. While they are invigorating the antiquities market, the amount of additional material could cause a drop in value over all. There's some concern this could trigger a large-scale disruption in the economy. If I remember, most of the pieces are Egyptian, small, rare, and of high value."

Samir clapped his hands together. "You've made good work of your free time in the air on the trip from Amphyra to Londinium." He smiled and glanced over at his wife.

Kassandra immediately relegated him to the usual passel of insipid officials she dealt with; his wife on the other hand was of a different nature. Her eyes never strayed from Kassandra, constantly measuring and watching. It could very well be that Samir might require protection. If so, he'd married well. The lady in scarlet was someone to keep an eye on.

"So, I expect there will be some pieces in tonight's auction worth our attention?" asked Kassandra.

"Not just the offerings, but also those who are there to bid on them bear watching." Samir pulled his suit front down and made to run a hand across his hair, but Eileena caught it before he could. She gave him an understanding smile.

Their carriage came to a rocking stop and Kassandra steadied herself with a hand on the rail. A thumping overhead signaled the cab driver exiting his seat to open the door. He offered a hand first to Eileena and afterward reached for Samir. Kassandra took the moment to look about the interior and noticed something on the window close to her. There was a handprint there. A frost etched outline on the glass. Oddly, the outline of one of the fingers was broken on either side, the ring finger. She wanted to look more closely, but the cab driver was now reaching for her. She allowed him to help her down.

They had come to a stop in front of an impressive building, its stone ramparts towering over her like a castle. Samir pointed at the edifice. "In the past, this was the prison for Londinium, but as larger quarters were needed, it was renovated and sold to the auction house of Chime and Erinwyck. I am certain they felt that if you could keep the criminals in, you could also keep the criminals out, since their wares are rather expensive." With that he giggled and Kassandra liked him even less. His wife's attention was split between observing the exterior of the building and Kassandra.

She felt her eyes being drawn up the walls to the dark murder holes and arrow slits. Strange remnants from another time. But, Kassandra considered, this was all about remnants of older times that had strange histories. "Onward?" she suggested and stepped out of their way. The couple preceded her past the two guards at the door, who'd stepped aside upon the presentation of a sheaf of papers by the driver. Kassandra couldn't help but notice a glimmer of silver pass hands as well. A bribe perhaps. She took another look at the driver as surreptitiously as possible. Could he be a Directorate operative? Kassandra found that he'd disappeared like a shadow before she could enter the long hallway that led to the interior. Take off that dark cap, coat, and scarf and he'd be unrecognizable from the other men gathered here.

As she removed her gloves, the silk snagged briefly on the golden moebius twist ring she wore in remembrance of her mother. Free of the glove, it grew briefly cold. She glanced about looking for evidence of a passing spirit, but saw none. Shrugging, Kassandra entrusted her fur-lined coat into the keeping of the matron at the counter and gave herself a once over. She certainly wasn't as well dressed as most of the folk that chattered in groups here and there. She caught the eye of her hosts, then proceeded across the circular foyer to them. Eileena caught a champagne flute from a passing tray and passed it to her. When the other woman leaned close to Samir to laugh at one of his all too constant little jokes, Kassandra swiftly swapped it for a different glass from a passing waiter with a wink. Caution was definitely the watchword here. She sipped briefly and at the earliest opportunity exchanged it for a discarded glass.

She did give Messieurs Chime and Erinwyck this; they'd done their best to conceal the former nature of their building. Large potted palms and arrases broke up the shape of the rooms. Mirrors gave the impression of larger spaces. The sweet sound of a bell broke through the conversations. With that, the assembled crowd made their way into the interior.

The large common area was filled with chairs and an auctioner's block, complete with podium and gavel, was situated at the front. Several mirrors and lanterns allowed additional light to be focused on the block. Kassandra was surprised to see her hosts heading to a stairway on the right side that led to a horseshoe-shaped balcony overlooking the auction area.

When she'd climbed the staircase, Kassandra realized the galleries that occupied this level were once prison cells whose walls were breached to create larger spaces. Within lay some of the treasures displayed before the upcoming auction. Samir's eyes glittered at the wealth before him. He indicated a gold-decorated statue of a cat resting on a pedestal, just past three small wax-sealed jars crowned with the head of a jackal. He studied it intently from both sides, leaning far enough over the rope that one of the guards on the level edged a little closer. Eileena snaked an arm through his and drew him back. That gave Samir enough time to fish a monocle out of his jacket pocket and once again begin his perusal.

"Is that Bast?" Kassandra asked, stepping up.

Samir took advantage of her blocking the guard's view and leaned forward once more. Eileena gave Kassandra an eye roll and hooked two fingers through his belt to keep him from over-balancing. "Yes, my dear, you are quite correct. Note the eye of Ra and the scarab inlayed in gold on the collar, as well as the gold earring. All very typical of such a piece. Now were I to actually be able to touch it I might find some indication of the maker. We've quite a table of established patterns that indicate specific makers and, in most cases; the mark on this item should match one. But that's the problem. You see when the ships carried the survivors of the Death from the old world to New Britain there was only so much room for treasure. When the plague wiped out everyone in Europe and beyond, the escaping ships were filled with people and supplies and not much else. So in theory, we know exactly how many of these pieces should exist. They should all have histories and lineages just like your family and mine. It is most distressing."

Eileena noticing another approaching guard and hauled her husband backward. "It's both good and bad news for Samir. Extra work authenticating these new items but also if he does say they are real and they have no history, then it makes him look like he's been paid to lie. That leads to distrust and less work for him."

"So, is someone manufacturing these, are they-" Eileena's hand covered Kassandra's lips swiftly as the lady in red turned and nodded to the passing guard.

She turned back to Kassandra withdrawing her hand. "A thousand pardons. Just as some things are not done in polite society, calling an item for sale a... well let's just say perhaps, replica, isn't done here. You're impugning the reputation of the House and it's best to remember we are all guests here."

"My question does stand though," Kassandra continued.

"Then they are bloody magicians and everything I've been taught is useless," Samir snapped and availed himself to another glass from a passing waiter. "The aging of the pieces is the most difficult aspect to recreate."

"In consideration of all of these facts, I must admit I am still somewhat in the dark as to why I am here. My talents could be more useful elsewhere."

"I am afraid we've been rather focused on the aspects dealing with my husband's work. I'm sorry, that does tend to happen in these circumstances. However, there's been quite a bit of death associated with both the buyers and purveyors of these pieces. Then there are the fires. At every place a death has occurred there's been a fire, almost as if they'd spontaneously combusted! It was hoped that you might perhaps gain contact with one of the departed and acquire more information.

"Of the fifteen purchasers of these new finds, four are dead of mysterious circumstances. Two of the team that transported them to the auction house have gone missing and one from Samir's firm, well, all they found were his ashes. It's almost as if there were some mysterious curse." Eileena relayed that with raised eyebrows and then snatched the champagne flute from Samir and tossed off its remnants in one swift motion.

The bell tone sounded again and the Alhambras began to move toward the balcony where they could observe the proceedings below. As she followed, Kassandra heard a step behind her. But when she swung about the area was empty. Was someone from beyond trying to make their presence known? She thought back to the frost-limned handprint on the window. Then Eileena swept up beside her and grasped her arm to lead her to the wooden railing. She put herself between Kassandra and Samir and leaned out over the space, to point at the gathered folk below.

"The gray-haired fellow there in the ash-colored suit is Alfred Bontaire. Likes Roman and Greek pottery, as well as weapons, but has recently fallen for the same Egyptian fever as the rest of them. Two rows up is the secretary for Maxim Prohas, Rue Johanson. She'll bid as his proxy and is another one after tonight's offerings. Louis Cartier will be watching things closely. Poor boy's almost as blind as a bat; see the opera glasses they've given him. On the other side is Mademoiselle Lufait, trustee child of the family Lufait. She's probably hoping someone's been hiding a canopic jar in amongst things. A bit into the death fetish, I fear. Finally there's Desmond Hill. Can't really tell you why he's as taken with Egyptiana as the others, but his horse ranches in the Oxfordshire hills keep him in money." With that Eileena drew herself back and tipping her head to one side considered Kassandra. "So who do you fancy?"

Reflexively, Kassandra started backward away from the odd question. "Whatever do you mean?"

Sighing, Eileena turned back to the crowd below. "Who do you think is going to die next?"

She'd been asked quite a few odd questions before, but this one was new to Kassandra. "That's a bit outside of my parvenu. I speak to the dead, that's my talent."

The other woman rolled her eyes. "Of course you do, my dear. But where's the fun if you don't speculate? Samir is leaning toward Rue. I think he feels it has something to do with that awful name of hers. As for me, I would like to see the confusion that would occur were Desmond to drop over." She chuckled deep in her throat and waved over the waiter once more.

Kassandra was put off enough by all of it to snatch a glass herself. *Perhaps,* she thought, *it is time to steer the conversation somewhere else.* "Samir, given that the items are approved for sale, was there anything in common about them when you certified the lot?"

Samir's eyebrows and eyes rolled upward as he considered. "They were clean."

"What?"

"Look, when an item is brought in, we typically do a professional cleaning. If it's dusty or dirty, the residue provides a background as to the provenance of the item. Sand, of course, is very good when we are dealing with Egyptiana, especially if it is ground in. That can also be added, since we're being suspicious." He waved his hand briefly in front of him as if chasing away the notion.

"But there was nothing else consistent about any of the items?" Kassandra pursued the thought farther.

Samir leaned behind his wife, as if sharing a secret, "Well, it's just something I noticed and is most likely nothing, but of the pieces that I dealt with, there was a light scent of smoke and ash. Barely there, but since you mentioned it, I noticed it on more than one piece. I could be wrong of course; it was just something that occurred to me after you continued to ask. I was much more focused on where they came from. They must be from a collection that was brought over in secret, that's the only reasonable explanation."

"What about unreasonable explanations?"

"Surely you're not suggesting that someone is foolish enough to be tomb-raiding in the old world. Turning over the ashes for treasure and risk raising the Death once again? A disease that kills swiftly with no cure is the best no-trespassing notice I could ever imagine. The horror stories of Edward the Black conquering the Mexateca with the Death that he'd brought over in secret and unleashed are bad enough. You might as well tell me that they are from some lost treasure ship sunken off the coast." Samir snorted into his drink.

Kassandra looked at him over Elieena's corseted back as the woman leaned forward once more to wave at someone below. "If you believe they are real, then they come from somewhere and that's the most important question at the moment."

"Funny, I would have thought that 'how do I stop more people from dying?' might be a tad bit higher on the agenda. Look, Samir, it's Isobel. Wave to her," was Eileena's acerbic reply.

As the two waved to a woman in a deep green dress, Kassandra fumed. She took another sip from her glass and considered the gathering below. She'd forgotten to look for their driver. Her nose twitched. Did she smell smoke? Once again she felt a presence near her. Turning her head revealed the area was empty. If it *was* smoke, did that mean that one of the unfortunates who'd caught fire was seeking her out? Or did it tie back to what Samir had revealed concerning the scent of the artifacts? The sound of the auctioneer's gavel striking the podium drew her back to the events below. The sale was beginning.

Swiftly, the auctioneer worked his way through the first series of items with a flurry of bidding from the crowd. His voice rang out, the words almost running together in their cadence. Kassandra found herself mesmerized by the sound and shook herself into focus as Eileena pointed a finger at Rue to indicate that she'd won a bid for her master. The champagne. It must be the champagne, Kassandra certainly was not used to it.

Setting her glass down on a nearby table, she noticed that several of the Auction House workers were loading the pieces Samir had perused onto a wheeled cart. The gold on the figure of Bast winked as the piece wobbled when the cart was run off the edge of the carpet at the end of the landing. Before it was the same small jar. Kassandra wondered if it was a canopic jar of the type Mademoiselle Lufait was pursuing. Then her attention was redirected as the workers pulled aside the curtain to reveal a door that led to what she assumed was a dumb waiter. It would make sense, there was no way that they could get that cart down the stairs. It would be interesting to note the reactions of the guests to these pieces.

She noticed that her hand was slightly sticky from the champagne and Kassandra drew out her handkerchief to wipe it off. Afterward, she considered the small square of silk. The hairs on the back of her neck stood up once again. Her spirit guest was still with her. Perhaps she could use that to her advantage.

She rubbed the silk against the wool of her skirt until it started to bunch and crackle with static. Then she reached her hand out and contrived to accidentally drop the piece of material over the edge. "Oh," she said leaning forward, "that was clumsy of me."

"At least it wasn't a glass," offered Samir, with a faint roll of his eyes as if he couldn't believe her foolishness.

Eileena, on the other hand, was watching her intently. "Indeed."

Below them, the silk drifted on its way to the floor, occasionally moving to and fro based on what most would believe were small currents of air in the room, but that Kassandra knew was the influence of her mysterious spiritual benefactor. It eventually came down above the shoulder of a man with dark hair. He glanced upward and snatched it from the air. Kassandra met his gaze. *Got you*, she thought, *there's our driver*. His gaze narrowed briefly. and then, shoving the silk into his breast pocket, he turned back to the auction as though he was merely annoyed by the interruption. At that point, Kassandra focused on him, occasionally remembering to sweep over the others with her glance. Causing a small disturbance, the auction workers brought the cart along side the seating area and began unloading the materials onto the side table.

Mademoiselle Lufait gestured to one of the assistants with her fan, indicating the table. The woman came to stand next to her and listened as Mademoiselle continued to point insistently at merchandise on display. Eileena chuckled low in her throat, her eyes alight. "At last some entertainment. Lufait has noticed her prize. The things she'll get up to if she wins that. But first she'll want a good look to be certain."

"What do you mean?" asked Kassandra.

Eileena gave her a knowing grin and leaned closer to whisper, "She's part of a group that believes in ash bathing. Thinks that the dust of a dead Egyptian will take away years. She's just starting to gain some lines on her face, so recently she's grown desperate."

Kassandra did her best to try to keep the horror she felt from her face. She didn't think she succeeded particularly well since Eileena's expression grew sly. A loud pop brought them both back to the moment and they turned in unison to stare at the events unfolding below. Mademoiselle Lufait hadn't waited for the auction; she'd wanted to inspect the wares immediately. Wax scattered across her dress and over those seated near her. A puff of ash rose up in a small cloud and she began to cough. Everyone was frozen in fascination. Everyone except the cab driver, Kassandra saw him reach into his jacket and pull forth a round sphere. As the others around her also began to cough from the expanding cloud of ash, Mademoiselle continued her fit, now doubling over with great wracking heaves. When she briefly leaned back, the kerchief she'd covered her mouth with was spotted heavily with blood.

That was enough for the driver; he drew back and threw the sphere across the room against the wall beneath the balcony where Kassandra stood. She glanced at the large mirror on the wall and could see the sphere's contents spattered against the painting and tapestries there, which instantly burst into flame. The resulting explosion tore a large hole through the brickwork. She felt the floor tremble and the balcony she fell against started to waver.

That sphere was very familiar; in fact it reminded her of the explosives she and Cobham had found in the north when they'd investigated a downed dirigible. Explosives that had passed into the hands of the Directorate for safekeeping and study and were now used at will, what did that mean she wondered? But she wasn't given time to consider. Below her, as the crowd pushed away from the blaze and cries of "fire" rose, the cab driver raced toward the table with the artifacts. He swiftly gathered up the remaining canopic jars and joined the crowd seeking the exit. Sparing her one intense glare, he proceeded to lay about him, throwing elbows and kicking to clear a path. She got one last glimpse of him when she was suddenly pushed from behind.

Once again her unseen assistant was looking out for her welfare. There was a cracking noise and a rumble as the floor of the landing began to tip toward the open center. She felt a shove, this time even more insistent. Then Kassandra realized; she was being pushed toward the dumb waiter.

Reaching out, Kassandra caught Eileena's sleeve and, hoping the woman would likewise grab hold of Samir, proceeded to pull her toward the end of the landing. Together they staggered across the uneven floor passing several settees and couches. Kassandra had a moment of inspiration and dropped Eileena's arm to begin pulling all of the cushions from the furniture. She then proceeded to kick them across the polished flooring until they came to rest before the dumb waiter. Eileena drug Samir bodily to the opening and after tossing in the cushions, threw out an ankle and tripped him so he fell headlong onto the padded floor. She jumped inside just as Kassandra leapt away from the flooring, which had begun to cascade into the room below.

Looking about, Kassandra found the cables that ran the dumb waiter. She considered their arrangement as she fumbled for Cobham's gift. The ebony-cased stiletto dropped into her fingers and when she squeezed it a six-inch blade shot out. Then she shrugged, looked at her fellow passengers huddled on the floor, and slashed through all of the ropes. She had a second to point the blade away from her as she dropped to her knees. There was an even briefer interval as the dumb waiter hung in midair before striking the ground, its sides crashing outward, roof lowering down.

Kassandra pushed Eileena and Samir forward out of the wreckage. They stumbled into a room lit by fire. The overhead balcony's supports and flooring continued to plunge to the ground. Showers of dust and sparks flew through the air. Kassandra led them away following the last of the remaining auction guests. She pulled forth her goggles and clapped them on her face hoping they would protect her eyes from the ash and smoke.

As she neared the doorway, Kassandra glanced back. Mademoiselle Lufait lie spread out on the floor. Falling sparks had lit the dead woman's dress on fire, flames leaping upward. Beside the body lay the jar, the jeweled eyes of Anubis winked in the firelight. With a shudder, Kassandra directed her hosts after the panicked guests filling the long hallway.

After what seemed like an eon, they came out into the winter night, the cold shocking them awake. Eileena broke out into a sudden coughing fit and everyone around her drew back swiftly, only Samir remained at her side. In the space that cleared,

Kassandra caught her breath and wits. When Eileena dropped her hand to reveal no blood, Kassandra brought forth a sigh of relief.

A tug on her sleeve caught her attention. She didn't even need to turn to know she would see no one there. Kassandra bit her lip as she considered the best way to escape the crowd. A rumble from the Auction House made everyone turn. Light blazed forth from all of the windows. The murder holes and arrow slits threw forth blood-red illumination as the fire took hold in earnest. As a whole, the crowd surged backward. Here was the chance Kassandra waited for. She pulled away from her patrons. Following the lead of her guide, she wended her way through the bystanders.

At that point Kassandra realized she was still carrying the open stiletto in her hand and swiftly stowed it away. Clattering through alleyways, she ran forward. Ahead of her, a dark-cloaked figure flickered in and out of sight, jumping like a flame, silver limned in the darkness. Her guide was leading her downhill. The harbor. She was going to the harbor. Kassandra turned a corner and stepped through the fog rising off of the water. Suddenly, the golden moebius ring on her finger grew cold. Had her mother's spirit returned after all of these years? That thought brought her steps to a halt. The shade returned to tug at her sleeve, then a cold hand slid in between her fingers, its grip chilling her.

It all came at Kassandra at once, all those years ago facing down Lahvoi in the tomb full of chained hands. She realized that her mother's hand was not only severed above the wrist but also burned about its end. She'd been so shocked then, she could have hardly noticed. Why had it come to her now? Fire once again. After all of these years why had Anastasia come to lead her? What did it all mean? Her mother's spirit tugged harder on her as a light flickered ahead of them. At the end of a long wooden dock, a figure swung a lantern back and forth. They'd found the driver. Kassandra strode forward; the answers lay ahead.

Once she reached the dock, Kassandra chose her steps with care. Despite the insistence of her mother, she moved forward cautiously, doing her best not to alert the cab driver of her presence. His tall form swayed back and forth, lit by the swinging lantern. He wore a gentleman's coat and blue trousers that would have matched the cabbie's uniform. He was leaner than she'd guessed. Then she felt Anastasia's shade let go of her hand and the other pushed ahead of her. The Directorate man turned around, some sense warning him of danger, but nothing could have prepared him for the apparition bearing down on him. He dropped the lantern and one of the two canopic jars gathered to his chest slipped free. They both watched in horror as it fell to the dock.

There was a hollow sound as it struck the wood. Fortunately, the worm-eaten boards were soft with saltwater and the impact did not destroy the container. The lantern fell to the other side, tipping the excess oil, making the wick flare up. That was all it took, the driver stepped back in fear. Except there wasn't any more dock for him to tread. For an instant, he hung there tipped backward. Kassandra shot forward, grabbing for his free hand. But his fingers had slipped into the sleeve of the jacket and all she grasped was material. Still she held on, digging her heels into the board that ran across the end of the dock. "I can't swim," he said, his eyes bulging as his head jerked from side to side.

Kassandra felt the presence of her mother at her shoulder, the chill running down her side. "You can talk though." She gave his sleeve a small tug and felt him slip within the jacket. His eyes drew off to one side looking at the dark water ten feet below them. "It doesn't look as if your boat is coming soon, so talk. Where did the jars come from?"

He glared at her for a moment and a frisson of fear ran through her. How long could she hold him like this? Already her arms were beginning to tire. Interestingly enough, her mother wasn't helping her hold him. Then he was coughing out words, "They're from a plague ship that crashed on the shore near Eastcaster. The folk there burned the wreckage when it came ashore just to be certain. Not everything burned, because it was soaked in saltwater. The cases of artifacts lay there for years until someone was brave enough to dig them up."

Kassandra considered that the truth. She'd heard of the plague ships. Vessels full of corpses that drifted the sea, their crews having perished during the crossing. Stories told that the Sargasso held many empty ships filled with bodies. Occasionally, storms would bring them ashore. She had an idea what lay in the treasure trove that the Directorate sought, but she needed to be certain. "What is in the jars?"

He glared at her and she shook him once again, staggering at his weight. It must have been enough, because he gave in. "The Directorate believes the Death in some form or other is sealed up in some of the canopic jars that were found. Hence the Anubis heads, the lord of the House of the Dead. The wax in the seals was redone, sealing up the contagion inside. We known that Edward the Black brought it with him somehow and this seemed like a reasonable method."

"And you'd use it like Edward, wouldn't you?"

"Pull me up!" he cried, "You can't keep holding me. I can see your arm trembling."

"What a weapon to use against the Southrons, right? Because we're not winning this cold war. We could have a victory the same way that Edward the Black did, by slaughtering thousands with a disease that could turn on us like a rabid dog!"

His face contorted with fear and he dropped the other jar to reach for her. It hit the water, bobbed there for an instant and then vanished into the depths. Anastasia's phantasm would have none his desperate grasping though. Kassandra's mother slapped away his questing fingers. Then stepping out as though the dock continued above the water, the spirit closed the distance between them, plunging her hand through his chest as though it were as immaterial as herself. Kassandra could only imagine that cold grip closing about his heart. His mouth gaped open and his head fell back. His eyes locked onto hers. Kassandra's hold faltered and the sleeve rasped through her numbed fingers. As the man struck the water, she stumbled backward, falling to the wood. There was a tiny motion in the darkness and the driver was gone. From where she sprawled, Kassandra kicked out and the canopic jar that rested on the dock flew off the end of the dock out over the water. In a second it was gone.

From the salt-caked boards of the dock, she watched as the cold evening wind flicked aside the specter's cloak. Anastasia wore the same soft jodhpurs that had always scandalized her husband, a tweed jacket, and sensible black boots scuffed and worn. Her face, lined with years of care, bore the same smile Kassandra always remembered. In some small part of her mind, she knew that her mother's spirit had just killed a man, but she was also fully aware that Anastasia had done what she'd always done, born the weight necessary to save the many. A moment later, Kassandra felt her mother grasp her hand and pull her to her feet. She clutched at the railing of the dock. For an instant a cold hand lay against her cheek and then Kassandra was alone in the dark.

She stood there for some time. The wind whipping at her, the sounds of the ships in their mooring echoing in the night. Then it came to Kassandra. The handprint on the window in frost had one finger with a break across it. She pulled off the moebius ring and stared at it. Anastasia had worn that ring on her left hand, her dominant hand's forefinger. Her wedding band was on her right hand. She'd been with Kassandra from the beginning watching over her. After all of these years she was back. Somehow Kassandra knew she wasn't going to just vanish again. Despite all that had happened, it brought a desperate sort of joy to her. She clutched the moebius ring to her. She still didn't know what had ultimately happened to Anastasia, but it certainly appeared that she'd gone in search of one of the crashed plague ships and never returned. Fire had caught her.

Kassandra sighed. Looking back across Londinium, the inferno that was the House of Chime and Erinwyck threw red and orange light against the surrounding buildings. How many other jackal-headed jars were out there? The others who'd perished in fires must have been foolish enough to open the jars, leaving the investigating Directorate operatives no choice but to scour away a weapon they couldn't control. Perhaps all along Anastasia was working to keep the jars from the Directorate. That certainly sounded like her mother, dedicated even after death.

It was time to go. Her hosts were waiting. Her story would be a bit hard to believe. The moebius ring had grown warm once again in her clasp. Slipping it on, Kassandra headed back toward Londinium, her weary steps echoing on the wood of the dock.

FROM THE INTRODUCTION TO
DANWORTH'S HISTORY OF KINGS

THE DEATH DID NOT CHANGE THE WORLD, AS IT WAS KNOWN SO MUCH as end it. While mankind survived many various plagues, pandemics, outbreaks, and even ordinary diseases, the Death, as it was named, was on a different level. While outbreaks of the Black Plague were horrendously fatal, the disease had a tendency to burn itself out. The Death on the other hand killed eight out of ten within three days of exposure. Of the remaining two, one was so weak that they often fell prey to other diseases or perished from inability to acquire food or water. The tenth victim was what made the Death so insidious. For up to a month, this person was a carrier and highly infectious. Traveling away from the horror of the effects of the disease upon others meant that there was a constant wave of expansion. Natural barriers such as mountains and seas could be overcome in that time and what would normally stop an outbreak was surmounted by the Death. Ships were found adrift with a few barely living survivors and the cycle began again. The Death felt inevitable. It felt like judgment. It felt like the end of all things, but fortunately some did not agree.

There are stories about the origin of the disease that place its beginnings in the frozen north. Accounts report that the horsemen of the steppes were the first to suffer and that even the swift passage of their mounts was not enough to escape the Death's reach, but rather aided in its spread. There are tales of dead horsemen, tied to their saddles to keep themselves astride their mounts in their illness that rode onto the lands of the Rus. From there the disease spread amongst its peoples. The Death flowed like a river through the Germanic tribes and south as well. It pushed a swell of the displaced before it as the news spread and the desolation was left behind. In 1366, word of the Death came to the court of Edward the III in Britain.

A portion of the country believed that the channel's separation from the continent would save them and were content to let the disease make an end of the rest. Fortunately, their leader saw things differently. He understood what they saw in the miles of water separating Britain from Calais. But he'd listened to all of the stories and knew that the ships of the dead that were found around the Mediterranean meant that the Death could survive for long periods of time. It would take a nearly insurmountable barrier to be safe from the Death—a barrier like an ocean. Without two people all Edward would have done was hope, but Jamison Maxwell and Demetrios Kapernak had the solutions he needed.

Maxwell was a collector of the unusual and had many strange books, scrolls, and maps. When he heard of Edward's hopes to escape the Death, he knew he had the answer. He presented the maps of Saint Brandon the Navigator to the king with one request. If Edward were to venture to the lands that Brandon described, then Maxwell would go with him. Partly it was to save himself and also to placate an unfulfilled desire for adventure. Maxwell was a name that would go down in history as a family of inventors and explorers who would leave their mark on the New World as well as help conquer it. It was his foresight that brought along the ancient document rumored to be stolen from the Library at Alexandria. A scroll that detailed a device called Heron's Helper, the very forerunner of the steam engines that would come to power New Britain. But like a promise, it would lay for many years before another of the Maxwell clan would bring it to fruition.

Demeterios Kapernak sailed his small fleet of seven ships out of the Mediterranean, away from the remains of his homeland of Greece. He passed the Pillars of Hercules and a great storm caught them up. The ships were pushed farther and farther off course until they came upon the shores of Britain. The men of Britain were familiar with the hulks and cogs of the time, but Kapernak's fleet was something different. Instead of the typical flat-bottomed ships these hung more sail and sat differently in the water. The caravels were a surprise and a timely one. These were the kind of vessel to cross the great expanse of water shown on Saint Brendan's maps. Like Maxwell, Demeterios was a man of vision and not only did he help in the building of the ships for the crossing, but he made them larger and more stable. He too made one condition for his aid. It was not one that the king could have foreseen. Demetrios required that Edward take as many as he could across the sea, turning none aside whatever their ancestry, unless they were infected. In the years that followed the landfall in the New World, Demetrios continued exploring further westward until he found the mouth of the great river known by the natives as the Mississippi. He founded his own city there, Amphyra.

If necessity was the mother of invention, then desperation was the force that wound the clocks that measured progress. What looked impossible when Edward first stared down on Brendan's maps fell beneath the keels of the ships of the exodus. There are many stories of the crossings. The first group of twelve ships that gained that far shore brought with them Maxwell and Kapernak. Together they both strode out onto that new beach and claimed the lands they found in the name of a New Britain and King Edward the III. When Maxwell set off to explore, Kapernak sailed once more for Britain. His next trip brought Edward and even more ships. In all, Kapernak made eight crossings before passing the task to his sons. By then the Old World had fallen. Only a few more ships would come across. Two of Kapernak's sons would never return. In the years that followed two cases of confirmed ghosts ships were recorded. The ships full of those killed by the Death were set ablaze with flaming arrows and beaches were quarantined thereafter. This was the closest that the Death ever came to New Britain. But there were rumors that not all respected the quarantines.

In the years that followed, Edward went north following Maxwell's explorations until he came to a great bay formed by a river that reminded him of the Thames half a world away. There he founded Londinium, set down a throne and ruled New Britain as King. His people met the inhabitants of these new lands. Some they befriended and some they warred with. On whole though, the immigrants were a desperate people and they took the lands from the natives. They pushed them ahead of them until they were forced across the Mississippi. The natives stopped north of Londinium and stood their ground. There they forged a peace with the Britains. Their coalitions of tribes made their homes in these lands and they kept their ways. In the end, the Britains turned their ambitions south.

Edward sent his brother with Kapernak's ships across the warm gulf waters to lands of the south and there he set about conquering all that he found. Eventually, he became known as Edward the Black. It was rumored that he even used the Death itself to defeat the tribes of the great stone cities of the south, to steal their gold, to take their lands and to bring them to their knees. While New Britain grew roads like the stretching branches of a tree, the lands to the south grew plantations of sugar cane, cattle, and ranches to raise horses. While the people were not enslaved, they were instead caught up in indentured servitude. As the plantation lords grew richer and richer, they kindled the fires of resentment.

For a long time that was how things remained. Edward after Edward ascended the throne. Each took the same name to honor the visionary who led from the old world to the new. Roads were built all across New Britain and mines were dug. Cities and towns grew up. The country filled out. Ian Maxwell puttering through his ancestor's holdings found the scroll of Heron. The first steam engines were built. Then the steam-powered ships ran up and down the Mississippi and about the coast. Railroads stretched across the country. Finally, airships and dirigibles took to the skies. It was a golden age for New Britain, an age that extended its beneficence to the south as well. Steam powered ships brought the cane and other riches to Amphyra where they flowed through out the empire.

But gold tarnishes with time and great nations fall. New Britain did not fail but rather withered. The focus of its people drew inward. The expenses of running the plantations grew and grew. The unrest of the servants increased. The rebellious inhabitants of the Southron islands encouraged the plantation workers to rebel. Instead of taking on this challenge, the military retreated. New Britain shrank, pulled in on itself.

The Edward kings did not give up. They built new weapons, trained new armies and formed the Councils of War, Welfare, and Trade to look after their people. Their people created the Directorate to watch over the kings. A fragile peace exists in New Britain with old enemies to the south and reluctant allies to the north. The new world is a second chance but it can be lost as easily as the old if its keepers are unwary

IN APPRECIATION

THANK YOU TO ALL OF THE TEACHERS, FAMILY AND OTHERS WHO TOLD me to keep writing. Thank you to the nerd family who keeps coming back to Watch the Skies to talk about books and all of the friends I've made from the conventions, events and late night conversations in the bar. Thank you to my Renfaire family who gives me a place to escape to when the real world ways too heavily upon me. Most of all, thank you to the folks at eSpec Books who made this possible: who kept saying "We'll publish a book of yours one day", who made sure the best words were in the right order and who brought Kassandra to life with that awesome cover. Finally, thank you to you, the reader. If you've made it this far, then thank you for coming along for the ride, hope you've had fun and I promise there are more adventures on the way.

JY

ABOUT THE AUTHOR

JEFF YOUNG IS A BOOKSELLER FIRST AND A WRITER SECOND – although he wouldn't mind a reversal of fortune.

He is an award winning author who has contributed to the anthologies: *Writers of the Future V.26, In an Iron Cage: The Magic of Steampunk, Clockwork Chaos, Gaslight & Grimm, By Any Means, Best Laid Plans, Dogs of War, Man and Machine, If We Had Known, Fantastic Futures 13, The Society for the Preservation of C.J. Henderson, TV Gods & TV Gods: Summer Programming.* Jeff's own fiction is collected in *TOI Special Edition 2 – Diversiforms* and the forthcoming *Spirit Seeker.* He also edited the *Drunken Comic Book Monkey* line, *TV Gods* and *TV Gods – Summer Programming.* He has led the Watch the Skies SF&F Discussion Group of Camp Hill and Harrisburg for seventeen years. Jeff is also the proprietor of Helm Haven, the online Etsy and Ebay shops, costuming resources for Renaissance and Steampunk.

MEMBERS OF THE
SPIRIT SEEKER SOCIETY

A. Eleazer
Aidan Schneider
Alla Lake
Allison Kaese
Amanda S.
Amy Matosky
Andrew Topperwien
Ann Stolinsky
Ann Wiewall
Anthony R. Cardno
Ashli Tingle
Barbara Silcox
Beth McNeal
Brendan Lonehawk
Bruce E. Coulson
Carl and Barbara
    Kesner
Carol Gyzander
Catherine
    Gross-Colten
Cathy Franchett
Cato Vandrare
Chad Bowden
Cheyenne Cody
Chris Cooper
Christopher J. Burke
Cindy Matera
Connie Brunkow

Craig Hackl
Curtis & Maryrita
    SteinhourYew
Dagmar Baumann
Dale A Russell
Dave Hermann
David Mortman
DavidZurek
Derek Devereaux
    Smith
Donald J. Bingle
D-Rock
Elaine Tindil-Rohr
Eric Hendrickson
Erik T Johnson
Erin Hudgins
Gail Z. Martin
    & Larry N. Martin
Gavran
Gina DeSimone
GMarkC
H Lynnea Johnson
Isaac 'Will It Work'
    Dansicker
Jacalyn Boggs
    AKA Lady Ozma
Jakub Narębski
Jasen Stengel

Jean Marie Ward
Jen Myers
Jenn Whitworth
Jennifer L. Pierce
Jeremy Reppy
John Green
Joseph R. Kennedy
Judy Lynn
Judy Waidlich
Karen Herkes
Katherine Long
Katherine Malloy
Kelvin Ortega
Kevin P Menard
Kumie Wise
Lark Cunningham
Linda Pierce
Lisa Hawkridge
Lorraine J. Anderson
Louise McCulloch
Margaret St. John
Maria V. Arnold
Mark Carter
Mark J. Featherston
Mary M. Spila
Max Kaehn
Michael
    D. Blanchard

Michael Fedrowitz
Mishee Kearney
Moria Trent
Myranda Summers
Nanci Moy
    & David Bean
Nathan Turner
Nellie
Nigel Goddard
Paul May
Paul Ryan
PJ Kimbell
Quentin Lancelot

Fagan
R.J.H.
Ralf "Sandfox"
    Sandfuchs
Revek
Richard P Clark
RKBookman
Robert Claney
Ross Hathaway
Sam Tomaino
Scott Elson
Scott Schaper
ShadowCub

Sheryl R. Hayes
Stephen Ballentine
Susan Simko
Tasha Turner
thatraja
Tim DuBois
Tomas Burgos-Caez
Tory Shade
Tracie Lucas
Tracy 'Rayhne'
Fretwell
V. Hartman DiSanto
Y. H. Lee

CPSIA information can be obtained
at www.ICGtesting.com
Printed in the USA
BVOW11s1527030518
515129BV00001B/8/P